I0521471

Luna Station Quarterly

Issue 026 | June 2016

Editor & Publisher

Jennifer Lyn Parsons

Assistant Editors

Tara Calaby
Cathrin Hagey
Andi Marquette
Dana Mele
Megan Patton
Danielle Perry
Iona Sharma

Cover Artist

Sara Kipin

LUNA STATION PRESS

Luna Station Quarterly publishes short fiction on March 1st, June 1st,
September 1st, and December 1st. For more information and submission
guidelines, please visit our website at lunastationquarterly.com

For Luna Station Press

Creative Director - Tara Quinn Lindsey

 LUNA STATION PRESS

576 Valley Road #197

Wayne, NJ 07470

www.lunastationpress.com

info@lunastationpress.com

CONTENTS

EDITORIAL

Jennifer Lyn Parsons

We have had a long-running column on our blog (you do read our blog, right? it's fab) written by Chloe N. Clark. Her column has focused on fandom studies, with an emphasis on fan fiction. Happily for her and sadly for us, the column has come to an end as she's earned her MFA and is moving on to some awesome new opportunities.

Her departure leaves a gap in the LSQ family, one that is vitally important to me. While I may not have the academic credentials Chloe does, I agree with her stance that fan fiction is a vital, important genre (medium?) within writing. Most of you who know me know I used to write Star Wars fan fiction. It's where I learned how to write.

Unlike many writers, I did not have the drive to tell stories in the traditional sense, from birth. As a child, my outlet was imaginative play, lots of running around the yard pretending a stick was a lightsaber, and getting the other kids on board with my ideas for new adventures for the characters I loved.

Then growing up happened and a lot of things got in the way of that vivid imagination I had when I was younger.

I had thought about writing a bit here and there over the years, but nothing really came together until Revenge of the Sith came out. The internet had grown up enough by then that TheForce.net and its forums existed and I was able to find a group of wonderful people on their fan fiction boards. I worked up the courage to write my very first story. It was... not horrible. I was helped a lot by the fact that I was well-read and a bit older than your average first time writer.

Just as important, though, was the wonderful concept of the beta reader. My first beta reader helped me by proofreading and talking through a couple of spots when I got stuck in the plot, as well as being an all around awesome cheerleader. Beta readers are a side benefit to writing in fandom that is not to be underestimated.

Also not to be underestimated? Feedback. There are few places an author can go to be guaranteed a warm response to their work. All writers want to see their work read by someone. We often start out telling the stories for ourselves, but they really feel like living, breathing things when they have someone read them. Beyond the ego boost, though, is the valuable skills a writer can develop in fandom.

Original work is important, but I have a habit now of telling new writers to think about starting their journey in fan fiction. Working in a world you are familiar with means you already love the characters and the setting and you won't get caught up in world building. This frees the author to focus on learning plot and structure. It also gives one the freedom to play with genre and form, from the ever popular drabbles and vignettes, to long form works that rival the source material for breadth and length.

While all those factors may give you a reason to start writing fan fiction, there is one more aspect to it that makes it a worthwhile endeavor, even when writing time is limited: it's just plain fun. Getting to write your favorite characters, tell wild, silly, sad stories, and then sharing them with the friends you make in that community is a priceless experience.

Hopefully I don't have to sell you all on the importance of fan fiction as a force in pop culture and an awesome place for new writers to cut their teeth. There are a plethora of articles on the subject, with the ability to back their claims up with centuries of examples.

All of that valuable experience is important to a new writer, but you may be wondering what all this has to do with LSQ. Quite frankly, if fan fiction did not exist, if I hadn't participated and found so many wonderful women writers through that community experience, LSQ would not exist.

I'm not honestly sure how much people know about what that community is really like. It changes over the years, 'ship wars come and go, but there seem to be a couple of consistent aspects that I find interesting and inspiring. For example, the vast majority of both writers and readers are women. These women come from all walks of life, all ages, all levels of experience. Some of them wish to become published authors, some already are published, and others just want to enjoy building onto and retelling the stories they love and being part of a community.

Fan fiction is all about love. Yes, sometimes it's about the expression of love that maybe you don't want your boss to catch you reading. But it's also about love of story and characters and their creators. That love of storytelling shines through with every lovingly crafted word.

It was in learning about these women and their wonderful, imaginative storytelling that I was inspired to start LSQ. I wasn't seeing the magic, the love, the sheer joy I saw in fan fiction out in the world. Everyone was always talking about original fiction as if it was a burden they had to bear, that telling stories was akin to opening a vein and it was horrible and don't do it. And yes, it can be challenging to tell difficult, painful stories, but underneath it all, there should be a thread of joy. My own experiences showed me there was another way, another kind of voice out there, that wasn't getting enough attention.

It was in seeking that thread of joy that I started the magazine you now hold in your hands. It was never something I ever foresaw myself doing and yet seven years later, here I am and here you are and here is another issue filled with stories that carry that intention forward. This volume is filled with tales that were a joy and a challenge for their authors to write.

Like so many things in our lives, one turn leads to another and another and before you know it, you can no longer extract a thing from its origin. Change just one aspect, just one choice, and the road leads in a very different direction.

After many unexpected twists and unplanned turns, for Luna Station Quarterly, that origin sits proudly in fandom.

Now go write something that brings you joy.

L S Q | o 2 6

SYCAMORE HEIGHTS

Josie Turner

Josie Turner lives in a small town
outside London, and works for
the National Health Service.
She has had fiction and poetry
published in a range of journals
including *The North*, *Crack the
Spine*, *The Fractured Nuance*,
and has a story forthcoming in
Emrys Journal.

In 2015 she was a joint winner
of *The Plough* short story
competition.

The Masons would not have booked their beds in advance. They were not that organised. Their journey towards the ferry terminal had been full of muddle and rage–Stuart Mason had sworn over the poor signage at every road junction, while his wife Laura muttered about all the things they'd forgotten–all the ointments and hairbrushes and face flannels and spare socks they'd failed to scrape together at six o'clock that morning, and would therefore need to buy, at great expense, once they reached the island.

Maisie Mason dozed on the back seat. Her parents' anger was never directed at her and, although she was the pretext for the holiday, they had both forgotten about her.

She had a growing sense that her parents were not like other parents. She guessed that other families planned for holidays, packed methodically, and set off cheerfully, smiling from car windows and perhaps even singing songs. She was beginning to suspect that her parents needed looking after–and that, one day, this would become her job.

They made it to the island, having caught the ferry with minutes–seconds–to spare. They had been the last car to arrive. Stuart had driven over the teetering ramp just as the barrier was lowered, and Maisie watched the metal pole slicing down behind the rear window, shutting them in. They were committed now, squeezed onto the car deck with hundreds of laughing, brightly-dressed families. They were going on holiday.

In the passenger seat, her mother shook her head from side to side, then dropped her head into her hands. "Oh God," she groaned. "Why does everything have to be such a nightmare?"

***

"Just look for 'Vacancies', will you?" Stuart hissed at his wife, steering the car between cloudy banks of meadowsweet. "It's not difficult."

"It is difficult when there are no buildings on either side of the road," she shot back. "Why have you driven into these fields?"

"Because there weren't any shitting B&Bs in the shitting town!" he yelled, raising his hands from the steering wheel. Dislodged, the long kinked hank of hair that covered his bald patch fell across his eyes. Maisie recognised the climax of the argument, which these days she followed like music. She sat white and rigid behind her mother, staring out at the furrowed acres of crops.

And then she saw a building. Tall and dark, on the edge of a field, with angular windows in its attic, like a row of pointed hats. Shuttered windows. It might have been a farmhouse, out in the middle of nowhere—and yet it didn't have the rounded edges of a farmhouse. No animals would ever snuffle around those walls; no hens would peck at corn thrown from its back door. No birds would fly overhead. Maisie could only hear the rustle of the car's wheels over the rough track, and the simmering silence between her parents.

'They'll miss it,' she thought. 'They'll drive straight past it.'

Maisie wondered if it was a house only she could see. Some

things were like that—cats and lights and certain trees appeared plainly to her, but she could not persuade others that they were real, and so she had gradually learned not to talk about them.

"There's a sign!" said Laura, pointing towards the house. It loomed large now, and Maisie could see that its window frames were painted in a charcoal grey.

The wooden sign swung from a cross -

*Sycamo*re Heights
Vacancies

That word, Vacancies, made Maisie's stomach sink. The V, followed by all the whispering C and S sounds: preceded by the hard C in Sycamore. It was like a poem, she thought, turning the words over and over in her head—or a spell, the sort of spell that makes the world fall away beneath your feet, leaving you stranded. Heights, she mouthed, feeling just as she had that time her class climbed the spiral staircase of a castle turret, the slippery stone steps dipping like water beneath their sandals.

Stuart gave a great subsiding sigh, and nodded that it would have to do. It was getting dark, and they needed to find somewhere. They needed to unpack, and have a meal, and unfold their maps; perhaps they were near the sea - perhaps this holiday might work out, against all odds.

Laura unclipped the passenger door and stepped onto the driveway of Sycamore Heights. Maisie immediately pushed the passenger seat forward and escaped from the car, slipping her hand into her mother's hand. Stuart was only her stepfather, and being alone with him made her feel queasy. She didn't like the way he looked when he took off his glasses to clean them on his shirt—his eyes protruded, and his long greasy hair fell in front of them, making him grumble, and push the hair back to the top of his head.

Laura squeezed her hand, and the two of them walked towards the shining grey front door.

***

"…and here comes a little girl!" said the woman who greeted them. "Hello, sweetheart!"

She bent down until her face was level with Maisie's. She was an old lady wearing roughly applied coral lipstick, as though she'd smeared it on at the approach of visitors. She had a hard mass of blonde hair all around her head, and there were silver rings on her fingers. Maisie found her intriguing. Old ladies were usually nice to her, and a reliable source of sweets and comics. She wondered if she could have a room to herself, rather than a camp-bed in a family room. She even dared to hope for a four-poster bed, covered in gauzy veils. She'd seen one of those in the castle.

The house was quite cheery inside. They had been ushered into a room crammed with painted plates and horse-brasses. There was a crocheted cloth on a round table, and on top of that slept a ginger cat which the old lady shooed off, before turning apologetically to Laura - almost as though her visitor was someone who cared about housework, and put coasters under mugs, and bothered about a bit of cat hair. The Masons' own house was inches thick in cat hair, and worse, and although they had a dining table it had disappeared years ago beneath an avalanche of plastic bags and broken appliances.

"The rates are twenty-five pounds per night for Mummy and Daddy," the landlady explained. "And only ten for the little girl. Including breakfast, of course. And I can always find a little snack, if needed," she winked, reaching out to pat Maisie's shoulder.

Biscuits, thought Maisie—this woman will supply me with chocolate biscuits. She followed the ginger cat with her eyes as it padded sleepily around the table legs—it looked a fat old thing, amenable to stroking. She hoped for a room at the top of the house.

"…I'll have to ask my husband," Laura was saying, in a wavering voice Maisie hardly recognised.

"Well, nothing to ask really, is there?" smiled the lady. "You won't find better rates anywhere, and I keep a clean house." She slid a potted poinsettia towards the centre of the table, to cover the place where the cat had slept. "And it's getting late."

"I'll just go and ask my husband," Laura repeated. She had thrust Maisie behind her. Suddenly she turned and marched Maisie along the cabbage-smelling hallway to the front door. There she grabbed the handle and pulled—and twisted—and then at last, although it could only have been a few seconds, she slid back a bolt and the door sprang open.

Maisie was pushed across the crunchy drive. She could see Stuart reading a paper he'd spread over the steering wheel of the car. Behind her, she heard her mother's shoes, pattering with a strange irregularity, as though she was dancing—and behind those steps, fainter still, an odd crawling sound, as though Laura's partner in the dance had fallen and was being dragged along.

All in one motion, Laura's hands siezed the passenger door handle, pulled it open, yanked the front seat and threw Maisie into the back. That was exactly it—she threw her, and Maisie landed sideways and astonished along the toffee leatherette. The car rocked as Laura jumped in the front.

"I can help with your things," the landlady was saying. She had followed them out, and now she stood holding the passenger door so that it wouldn't close.

"That's very kind of you," Laura was saying, and it sounded as though she was crying. Maisie was still seeing the world at an angle, as she lay winded on the back seat. The old lady's dirty silver rings were moving further into the interior of the car, like a dentist's instruments being inserted into a mouth. Laura was trying to tug the door shut. Thank you so much," she wept.

Stuart, very slowly, folded his newspaper.

"So," he frowned, as he watched the tussle. "Are we staying?"

"Drive!" Laura yelled, right in his face. "DRIVE!"

He gaped at her for a moment, reaching for the gear stick. Laura made a last desperate grab for the passenger door, which seemed to slam on the old woman's fingers as the car moved over the gravel. Maisie looked back to see her doubled over and clutching one of her hands in pain. She was shouting something towards the car. There was a lot of noise everywhere, and the house looked different, suddenly–small and white, like a cottage, with its windowsills painted jaunty colours.

Maisie felt her heart juddering in her chest. She knew she got a lot of things wrong: she saw things that weren't there, she got terrible headaches, and certain words made her feel ill. But now Mum was crying–great wracking sobs, and as she bent over the dashboard Maisie could see two long jagged rips in the shoulders of Mum's blouse, and the pale skin underneath speckled with dots of blood.

***

"I fail to see," Stuart was saying, as he pulled into a lay-by and braked abruptly. "I fail to see what this performance is about."

Laura hadn't said anything for twenty miles. She held a wet tissue to her face.

"You must have got tangled in something," he reasoned. "To tear your blouse. Hardly the lady's fault."

Laura didn't respond, except to take a deep inward breath.

The air in the car was nasty. They would have to sleep in there all night–Mr. and Mrs. Mason tilting their seats backwards, and Maisie stretching in relative comfort behind them. She would have to pee in the hedgerow, among nettles and cow dung. Their toothbrushes and pyjamas, if they'd remembered to bring them, would be jumbled in laundry bags in the boot.

It was surprisingly easy to fall asleep. Maisie wanted to lose the terrible memory of her mother's weeping. It gave her the same feeling of instability as those dipping steps in the castle had done; the feeling evoked by that word on the sign–Heights.

She closed her eyes and thought of the nice old ginger puss on the round table. As she dozed, she reached out a hand to his tufty fur. But he turned and hissed at her touch, and lashed out with his claws until her skin was speckled with blood. Roused from her dream, she opened her eyes to see the familiar orange stitching in the back of Mum's car seat. Her hand stung. She shifted, and went back to sleep.

***

"…we would never have got out. I know you don't believe me. But we would never have left that house."

"She seemed harmless to me–"

"You didn't see inside, Stu. All black and grey. Grey nets at the windows. It was like the ashes after a big fire."

"It looked pretty enough on the outside. Window-boxes–"

"Of course it did. To lure us in. But inside–oh, God! And she had a dead cat, Stu, on her dining table."

"…What?"

"It was dead."

"You mean stuffed?"

"No."

Then they both laughed–a dark, desperate laugh.

"Oh, what are you talking about, Laura? As if she'd have a–"

I'm telling you it's true–no, shh, you'll wake Maisie–stop it!"

The car seemed to rock with their laughter. They were always like this, in their moments of reconciliation–teetering on the brink of an hysteria more frightening than conflict. Maisie lay still in the dark, waiting for them to be quiet. She could hear the wind outside the car. There was no moon, no stars, but she could make out the movement of straggly trees at the side of the road, shielding them from occasional passing cars. She was thirsty, but she felt warm underneath her checked jacket. Gradually she eased off her shoes, using the toe of each foot to lever their backs.

A dead cat? Ashes? She closed her eyes. She knew she got a lot of things wrong.

***

"Shit. Shit!"

Stuart, still half-asleep, grabbed the steering wheel and turned the key in the ignition.

"Wha - ? What is it?" cried Laura, turning instinctively to look over her shoulder. Maisie lay in the nest of her jacket, one eye warily open. "It's alright, Poppet. Nothing to worry about."

The car bucked out of the rough lay-by, until its wheels gripped the tarmac of the empty road. Maisie propped herself up on one elbow to watch the needle of the speed dial flickering past sixty, then seventy miles per hour.

"Stu, for God's sake–what's happening?"

"Never mind," he muttered, easing his foot off the pedal a little. It was just before dawn, and a lilac light filled the air.

Behind them, on the horizon, Maisie could see a thin line of fire where the sun rose. The Sun is fire, she thought, and the Moon is rock. And the Earth is both, she told herself, thinking of all the volcanoes jostling underneath the skin of the world—under the lawns and houses and shopping centres, even under this road they drove on now.

Laura begged Stuart to slow down, to stop, but he drove for miles until they reached a caravan park, where a convenience store was rolling up its shutters for a new day. The three of them went inside and bought individual cartons of sugary squash, moving around the aisles on shaking legs.

***

It was a good holiday. Maisie kept a record of it in a notebook she'd saved for the purpose, with a hedgehog on the front cover and its pages faintly lined. The family visited an owl sanctuary and a stately home. Her favourite trip, though, was to a model village, which depicted tableaus from the island on a tiny but consistent scale, and even contained its own model village, which presumably contained an even tinier version, and so on to infinity.

"Isn't it clever?" Laura murmured, leaning over a section of the sculpture. "Apparently it started with a single village and kept growing. The whole island must be here. Think of the work that's gone into it."

"I don't know how they get it to scale," said Stuart, shaking his head in wonder. He looked around, as though to find someone in charge he could ask. "Getting it to scale's the hard part. I don't know how they—"

"Stu," said Laura, straightening up. "Let's go."

"What? But we're—what's the matter?"

"We have to go. Now." She was trying to keep her voice down. There were families all around them; couples with pushchairs, and elderly people leaning against railings. She was trying not to make a scene.

Maisie looked over to where her mother had been standing. That section of the sculpture was green, and flat, and boring. But among the green was a small grey spot, the size and shape of a Monopoly house. And if you looked closely –

"Come on, my girl," said Mum, hooking her arm and drawing her along the path. "We're going to the café."

Stuart trailed behind them, gesturing in protest at his wife's behaviour and looking for support among the indifferent crowd. Later Maisie heard him snarling "This has got to stop," and Mum snapping back at him, with a viciousness she seemed hardly capable of, that he hadn't damn well stopped that night, had he? In that lay-by? He'd driven off like a scalded bloody cat. And then she clapped her hand over her mouth, and Maisie guessed that the bad word had been 'cat'.

***

Their return ferry crossing was at six a.m.–a terrible hour. The Masons were late risers. At weekends Stuart would lie-in until teatime. As a family they preferred things to be almost over–days, outings, concerts, holidays. They liked the sense of having survived an ordeal, and of being able at last to return home, however unsatisfactory home might be.

"We'll find somewhere near the terminal," said Stuart, as though he'd planned it all along.

"Another Bed and Breakfast?" asked Laura. "That might be expensive." They had run low on cash two days earlier, and were eking out supplies from the boot of the car. Stuart had a credit card, but that was for emergencies, and it had worn a groove in his wallet with dis-use.

"No, no," he said airily. "We don't want all that fuss.

Disturbing people at an ungodly hour. We'll sleep in the car, and then we can be independent."

Being independent was the great thing for the Masons. It would have been their family motto, inscribed on their coats of arms.

But Laura went quiet at the thought of sleeping in the car again. She knew they had no choice, but she tried to think of an alternative, or at least a safe place to stay. Perhaps they could go back to that nice caravan park, which was full of loud families, where they held nightly discos in a corrugated shed?

Stuart sneered at the thought.

So they spent the last night of their holiday in the car, with Maisie stretched out on the back seat as before. Stuart steered off the road and found a clearing in a copse—when night fell, and the traffic lessened, they might have been in the middle of a primeval forest, so dark and dense were their surroundings.

***

Mr. and Mrs. Mason fell asleep almost immediately. His hank of hair slid backwards and dangled above Maisie's foot— she raised one toe and dared herself to touch it. He disgusted her, she realised. The breath that came out of his lungs became the air she inhaled into her own.

A sudden wind had started outside, and by the meagre illumination of passing headlights Maisie could see the shuddering trees. She thought about all the strange things that had happened, but mostly she thought about school, and whether she'd be allowed to get her ears pierced soon. She was conscious of keeping her thoughts under control, as though if her mind wandered too far to the left or right it would find something it could not contain.

In the morning Stuart would drive them to the ferry terminal, and then they would be free, she told herself.

She decided not to sit up and look out of the back window of the car.

Not ever to do that.

She would lie still with her eyes closed instead.

***

She turned and sat up very gradually. The night looked strange–not at all like a night framed by a bedroom window. She was in it, somehow, as though the car was a leaf being tossed among the highest branches of the trees.

No shelter, she thought. No protection.

In the darkness she saw a small patch of utter darkness. It had a shape, and a feeling, and Maisie thought that it was in pain. She screwed her eyes closed and lay down, down on the seat, trying to press herself into the springs and the webbing. The shape mustn't look at her, she knew that. She had to make herself invisible to the shape–something utterly beneath its notice, like a stone or an insect, not the guilty thing she was.

Not the girl who had seen those silver rings sliding into the car's interior.

Not the girl who'd seen blood pearling on her mother's back.

There was no sound but the wind, and yet she knew that the shape came closer. It could look in through the windows, if it wanted to.

Maisie pushed a toe into the back of Stuart's seat. He lay unmoving, his mouth open, his weak lower jaw ebbing into his collar. Her mother, next to him, resisted the hand Maisie pressed against her spine. They both lay as though dead.

Something leaned down hard against the back fender, and then let go, making the car rock.

Again.

Again.

Maisie fell through the gap in time between one exertion and the next. Over and again the car was pressed downwards, with a conscious malevolent force, and even as it jerked upwards her parents slept, perhaps dreamlessly, perhaps believing that the danger had passed.

***

"You're quiet, Poppet," said Mum, as the car nosed into the traffic queue. "Sleep well?"

Maisie nodded. The light was golden, ambrosial, all around and inside the car. The ferry terminal was the most beautiful sight Maisie had ever seen. Cellos seemed to play. It was over, whatever it had been, and there was no need to frighten her parents now. She would spare them. She looked at them compassionately. Being a grown-up was so frightening already.

Mr. and Mrs. Mason were chatting about finding a coffee up on deck as their car slotted in amongst all the others. Maisie had a warm sense of communion with the people she saw around her. Children were pressing their faces against car windows, or grizzling, and parents were arguing with the same grinding trapped loathing that arose sometimes between her own. We're not so odd, she thought. Not so freaky.

She looked out of the back window, letting her petrified neck muscles relax. She sat up properly and took a good look, feeling that she'd conquered the morning. Their car rested high up on a curve, so she could see down the ramp to where the other cars trundled on, like slow gentle beasts—like the hedgehog on her notebook.

And then she saw the stumping shape, moving between cars. A patch of utter darkness against the light, walking where no person should walk. Bent over, as though in pain, and moving in a strange loping dance. The men in yellow jackets waved more cars on, as though the shape was not there.

Maisie felt her feet slip on those remembered stone steps; she felt herself plunge into insubstantiality.

As the ramp rose behind the last car, sealing the deck before the ferry set off, Maisie thought she saw a flash of silver in the darkness.

TO GIVE BIRTH TO A DANCING STAR

K B Sluss

KB lives in North Carolina with her kid, her husband, the occasional in-law, and a very hairy husky. She loves to read and has a sweet tooth for speculative fiction. She is a first reader for *Daily Science Fiction* and she has published short stories at *Daily Science Fiction*, *Everyday Fiction*, and *Stupefying Stories*.

Dr. Mai Pham wasn't looking for music when she found it fossilized in an Antarctic glacier. She had been collecting and analyzing ice core samples for data about Earth's prehistoric climates when she uncovered the relic. It was buried among the remains of a shattered meteor.

Protocol required Mai's team to prepare samples from the larger ice core and seal and maintain the specimens under controlled conditions. Despite the team's precautions, ice relaxation from drastic pressure changes weakened one sample. The ice shattered and released a blizzard of discordant sounds that ricocheted against the walls of Mai's subzero laboratory. The noise rang out as though a symphony of notes had leapt from a rooftop to crash in a disharmonic wreck on the ground below.

Mai's assistant attributed the phenomenon to abnormal frequencies transmitted by the research station's radio equipment, although none of it was in use at the time. "Don't think too much of it," he said. "Antarctica is notorious for unpredictability. Stranger things have happened."

That night Mai woke with the strains of a strange melody vibrating in her throat and it hummed between her lips. She rolled over in her bunk and tried go back to sleep, but a tickling sensation in her subconscious prevented it. Like a scratchy tag in the collar of her thermal undershirt, the music nagged at her and refused to be ignored.

She shed her warm cocoon of bedcovers and instead donned subzero gear then left her personal quarters and followed the subterranean hallway that led to the frozen work station. The exercise and cold air cleared the sleepy cobwebs from her mind, making way for logic. *What am I doing?* she thought. *What the hell do I expect to find?*

Mai unwrapped an ice core slice she had processed the day before. The sample came from the same section as the piece that had shattered. She cut away several thin wafers and prepared them for gas chromatography and mass spectrometry analysis.

The test results revealed a high concentration of silicon carbide, attributable to the presence of meteoric debris. Nothing in the data explained yesterday's anomaly. She studied the specimen again under her microscope, but discovered no microbial orchestras. She tapped the ice on her work table and held it close to her ear like a tuning fork. The sample silently ridiculed her experimentation, but it did not sing.

Mai cleared away the specimen and shut down the machines. Her hand lingered over the light switch as she paused at the doorway exiting the lab. Research demanded discipline and did not tolerate flights of fancy. And yet...

Her fingers drummed on her thigh. They tapped out a measure, an organized composition of yesterday's disordered notes in the way she might have played them on her piano at home--the same measure she had hummed when she first woke up. The tune was nothing she had heard before, but it spoke of logic, structure, and reason. It embodied order and harmony. It compelled, and the curiosity of it drove her forward.

Mai turned on her heel and went back into her lab. She

prepped a recording app on her cell phone and retrieved an ice sample from storage. She set the ice on her work table, letting its temperature rise until expansion wreaked its destructive havoc.

Among the mundane crackle of breaking ice, the unmistakable notes sang out again: discordant pulses--a cacophony, primordial and raw. When she listened to the recording captured by her phone, the sounds released from the broken ice affected her the same way her husband's saxophone had taken hold of her the night she first heard him play.

Before she returned to her room, Mai marked the lab's inventory records to indicate the piece had succumbed to ice relaxation. She hoped no one ever questioned her notes, because each of those samples was priceless--not for mere cost or potential profit, but for the insights they provided about a Time before the existence of man. Yet she had destroyed the sample, simply to collect a momentary burst of incomprehensible and indefinable data.

And if I had the chance, I would do it all over again .

***

Theo Spader's music suffused the interior of the little bar, hidden in the basement of a restaurant near campus where grad students went to drink retro cocktails and indulge in self-importance. Theo's saxophone pleaded like a lover begging for satisfaction as his elegant fingers fluttered over its keys. Mai shifted on her bar stool, crossing her knees, uncrossing, seeking relief from the way her body reacted to both music and musician.

Later that night, after gin rickeys and vodka gimlets, after Mai stumbled to Theo's apartment, tucked away from the cold beneath the crook of his arm, Theo called Mai his Angel Glow from a lyric in his favorite jazz song. She thought a man who breathed passion and performed musical sex for a living probably called lots of girls his Angel Glow, but when Theo kissed her and played her with his expert fingers, the things he said to other girls no longer mattered.

Before Theo came along, Mai believed jazz was the musical equivalent of francium, the most unstable element, which was radioactive and fractionate. Jazz notes were frantic, random, and willful. She thought that was also the perfect way to describe the sax player who stole her heart. Like a child after the Pied Piper, she followed Theo and his music, and she succumbed to the enticement of their chaos .

***

Mai's Internet research led her to the work of several Cal-Tech scientists who had experimented with nanoscale phononic crystals. These optomechanical crystals used tiny energy traps to capture quanta of sound waves within their structures. And silicon carbide--the stuff composing the ice core's meteoric debris--was an ideal material in which to develop these isolators.

The shattering of her samples may have provided the energy necessary to release vibrations trapped within the meteoric fragments, she theorized. Liberated sound waves pulsed through the ice shards and made them sing. But it wasn't a hypothesis about the physical possibility of these sounds that kept her from sleeping at night. The thing troubling her most was the insidious melody.

Long before her tenure in Antarctica, she discovered, a group of astronomers had come here to study the early universe. They attached a microwave telescope to a balloon, launched it into the stratosphere, and let it circumnavigate the South Pole for almost two weeks. Patterns in the resulting images confirmed that sound waves raced through the early universe, creating the structures that evolved into giant clusters and super-clusters of galaxies. Sound waves compressed and expanded matter and light, similar to the way sound waves compress and expand air inside a woodwind instrument.

The astronomers identified the waves' harmonics. Using musical analogy, they determined the pitches of the harmonic peaks. They called their findings the music of creation. The voice of God when He said, "Let there be light." The echo of the Big Bang as galaxies and stars and planets exploded into being.

If music had created the cosmos, Mai thought, *it would have been patterned and orderly.* She knew recreating the original arrangement from the current jumble would require patience, stamina, and perhaps a little providence.

It would also demand the application of methodical reason and a meticulous removal of chaos.

***

In her bedroom at home, Mai clutched an unmarked box, not much larger than something sized to hold a piece of jewelry: a bracelet, or a slim necklace like the one Theo had given her when she first announced her pregnancy. The box rested in her palm, lighter than air, too light to contain so much agony. Her other hand curved over her hollow belly, much too hollow to have ever sheltered a life.

Her body was like lead. No, something heavier: osmium, the densest stable element. Except she wasn't stable. Her protons raged and her electrons careened, ricocheting off each other until she was sure she'd explode. *Please, God, let me explode.* On her knees, hunched over that goddamned box, Mai begged, *Give me my own personal Big Bang-- so many pieces of me.*

So many pieces racing so far apart that it's impossible to put me back together.

But she didn't explode and her body remained intact,

crystallizing into the frozen carapace that encom-
passed her pain.

She clutched the box until her fingers cramped into a cage
around it, and then she must have fallen asleep or passed out.
When she woke up, the box was gone and she didn't ask Theo
what he had done with it. After all, it wasn't a soul. It wasn't a
heartbeat or a flutter of movement inside her. It was nothing
but a container for miscarried remains, calcium phosphate
and trace metal residues.

Ashes and dust.

***

Mai emailed the digital recording of the shattering ice core
to Marco Dimetti, a technician from the studio where Theo's
band sometimes recorded. In his reply, Marco provided a
colorful report that displayed results from a spectrogram
analysis. It included individual pitches, the equivalent notes,
and the rate of occurrence for each note.

Mai, Marco wrote, *I don't know what this is, but it was hell
sorting it out. I separated everything and cleaned up the static.
If you get it straightened out, let me know. I'd be curious
to hear it.*

Marco had also separated the recorded sounds into individual bytes and uploaded them into a sequencing program
that allowed Mai to play with arrangement. Late in the
evening, after her laboratory shift, and after sharing a hur-
ried dinner with her colleagues, she logged into the account
Marco had set up online. She brought up the sequencer and
instructed it to play the ice core notes in the order Marco had
arranged them.

She cringed and stopped the playback soon after it began.
Honking horns in rush hour traffic made a better tune. She
hummed the first note of the refrain that had been haunting

her thoughts, then she played the sounds again, one at a time, until she found a match for the one repeating in her head.

The tune was elusive, a slippery fish evading capture. The more she chased it, the faster it squirmed away. She lacked many of the necessary pieces, and the task of constructing an organized composition despite those deficiencies overwhelmed her. After a while, and though she wanted to fling it against the wall, she quietly closed her computer, then put away her glasses, rubbed her eyes, and curled up under her bedcovers.

Mai defied defeat to claim its victory. Not yet. More ice core samples remained, hibernating in her laboratory. In their frozen depths lay possibility and potential, and those two words were the lullaby that sang her to sleep.

***

"It's just as well," Mai said. She sat on the edge of her bathtub at home, hands wedged between her knees. The contents of a home pregnancy test rested on the counter beside the sink. A minus sign radiated from the indicator, burning into the sky like a high-wattage spotlight, proclaiming her failure for the world to see.

Theo sat across from her on the toilet lid, his knees pressing into hers. A frown furrowed his brow and carved deep lines around his mouth. "Just as well?"

"It means I can accept that research position."

"Antarctica?"

She studied her bare toes as she burrowed them into the shaggy bath mat. *These fibers should be tickling my feet. The bathtub ceramic should be freezing my ass, even through these jeans. I don't feel anything, though. Everything is numb.*

"Antarctica," she said. "Yes."

"How long?"

"Eight weeks, give or take. Depends on the weather."

"You really want to do this?"

Mai looked into Theo's eyes--those same, questioning eyes stared into her every time the tests came up negative. She felt those eyes doubting her. They blamed, as if these failures were all her fault. *Maybe I'm being too sensitive, but probably not, she thought, because I blame him, too.*

"Yes," Mai said. "I think Antarctica is a good idea."

"When would you leave?"

"Six months?" said Mai. "Like I said, it depends on the weather."

***

After another night of surreptitious experimentation in her lab, Mai had captured a recording of the musical discharges of three additional specimens. Played back to back, the collection of sounds revealed subtle variations that indicated the presence of a wider array of raw materials. Again, Marco separated the individual sounds and uploaded them into the sequencer. He offered to replicate the missing tones by manipulating the pitches of the notes Mai had already captured, but she refused. Marco never asked why, for which she was grateful.

How could she say the melody whispered in her bones, infiltrated her DNA, and demanded precision? The music required notes gleaned from the source and anything else marred its perfection. The tune infected her cells and adhered to her atoms. Mai no longer knew if she was making the music, or if the music was making her.

The arrangement singing from the speakers of her computer resonated in the sleepy tones of a nocturne, but it still lacked a note--one solitary sound. The surrounding music revealed its shape in the same way an incomplete puzzle shows the outline of its missing pieces. Mai played the melody on repeat, and her imagination filled the holes with sounds from her dreams: a pitch matching the squeak of the rocking chair in her empty nursery; an arpeggio of a contented infant's cooing; a chord combination that mimicked the greedy purring of a baby at the breast.

***

Dear Mai,

How cliché is it that I'm writing you a letter? But I don't know how else to talk to you. Each time I try, you turn away. You act like you're alone in your grief and you refuse me the right to mourn him. How can you not see that I'm hurting, too?

Mai found Theo's note on her first day in Antarctica. He had buried it deep in her luggage and she thought he must have intended for her to find it after her arrival, after she unpacked and committed to the long stay.

You shut me out, and when you do talk it's only to tell me how much you hate everything I love. You've thrown out my records, banned me from rehearsing in the house, and you refuse to come to my performances. You blame my music for making you sick.

You lost your heart the day we lost our son. What a shame--you had an amazing heart, so full of music and warmth and love. In our house those were always the same things.

I hope Antarctica is the end of your quest. I hope you'll find peace there. You and that frozen continent have so much in common, after all. I suppose that's harsh, but I guess I'm beyond caring. I'm beyond all this now.

I'm done, living with ghosts.

On her bunk, with her bags half unpacked, Mai sat clutching the note in her fist, waiting for heartache, sadness, regret... something. In that moment she believed she could have walked outside with no coat, no mittens, no goggles. She would have survived because the ice would welcome her as one of its own.

***

Most of Mai's assessment techniques required controlled thawing, but a slow melt ruined the conditions necessary to release the music from the ice. So, she recorded manufactured data about elemental compounds and gas chromatography readings. She corrupted the sanctity of her research and defiled the purity of her scientific method for a single musical note. From pious to apostate, Mai betrayed her religion for this one, last thing.

As the final specimen crashed to the floor, Mai rejoiced in her irreverence. The shards crunched under her boots as she danced upon the ice.

***

Mai, Marco wrote in his final e-mail, *saw Theo at the studio. I told him what you were working on, your theories about music and conception. He said I shouldn't enable you this way. He asked me to stop working with you. But I'm a businessman. I've got bills and you pay upfront.*

So here it is--the final note you've been looking for. For whatever its worth, I wish you luck.

Mai started the playback, pausing the sequencer to drop this last, single pitched sound into the empty places lacking its voice. A perfect balance of rhythm, harmony, structure, and texture. The completed composition enveloped her skin. Her muscles quivered and her blood pulsed in time with the tempo. An orgasmic gasp and then a dense ball of intense heat permeated the abyss between her bellybutton and pelvis.

Deep inside her, a tickle of fizzing bubbles was replaced by the flutter of wings that transformed into the substantial movement of matter adjusting to the cramped space--the pushing and kicking of prenatal galaxies. The skin and muscles of her belly gave, expanding to accommodate increasing pressure.

This is it, Mai thought, *the music of creation. God's voice when he said, "Let there be light." The echo of the Big Bang as galaxies and stars and planets exploded into being.*

Labor pains mounted as the music ascended to its crescendo. At its peak, after a series of agonizing contractions, an out-pouring of light and heat expanded away from the singularity inside her, an explosive burst of primordial energy--her own personal Big Bang.

There are so many pieces of me.

So many pieces, racing so far apart...

DREAM CATCHER

Natasha Burge

Natasha Burge is a writer who divides her time between Bahrain and Saudi Arabia. Her writing can be found or is forthcoming in *Ink in Thirds*, *Tasa'ol*, *Flash Fiction Magazine*, and *Bitterzoet*, among others. She is currently pursuing a master's degree in creative writing and wrestling her first novel into shape. She has a tumbleweed heart, ink stains on her fingers, and one foot permanently planted in other words.

"The end."

I roll over and peer at Mei in the dim morning light, hoping the bounce in her dreamspool will fix itself and I can try to get some sleep.

"The end."

Sitting up with a sigh, I flick on the light and drag my toolkit out from under the bed. "Don't worry, sweetie. I'll fix it."

Mei blinks at me, her eyes unfocused as she bounces again and again through the final moments of her dream. Last time she bounced, she was in the massage dreamspool, and the masseuse had just reached the tight spot in her left foot, so while I was unwinding the cortical spools from behind her ear and flushing the ducts, she was writhing in my arms, a bleary smile on her face even as she asked for help.

This time it is an easier job; there is nothing wrong with the spools, just a loose dermascrew that I fix in seconds.

Mei yawns and stretches her arms overhead as she comes fully awake. "It was the old-style steak and mash. I'm still drooling."

Dream Catchers can hold eight dreamspools; you've got your standard moonlit beach, mountain sunset, laughing with a group of friends, hiking in a peaceful park, singing around a campfire, and a delicious meal, among others. The steak and mash is Mei's favorite.

"The only problem is the satiety factor," Mei continues, climbing out of bed and shuffling into the kitchen. "Dreaming about a steak that good and waking up hungry is a nightmare."

But, of course, it isn't really a nightmare because those didn't exist anymore.

"Thanks for the help, Ro. Sorry I woke you up," she says with another yawn.

"I was already awake," I mumble, sliding away the toolkit. I had been dreaming about my grandfather again, seeing his face, dark as oiled sand, peering out at me from my own mind. Before I can change my mind, I get out of bed and begin packing.

Mei prepares us a feast for breakfast; cooking is one of the few things she still does with something approaching passion and the synth-bacon almost tastes like actual meat. She is finished complaining about the bounce now, and I know better than to start in. To Mei, complaining about humanity's greatest achievement is incomprehensible, just as it would have been to me before I started seeing Guman's face in my dreams.

Nine years ago, the dreams of every person on earth stuttered to a halt and no one knew why. It was known as Oneiric Collapse and in a matter of weeks the ancient rhythm of life had come unmoored. Before OC, we woke up, lived our lives, and went to sleep to enjoy a cushion of time that wasn't quite ours, that wasn't quite real, and that most of us took for granted. After OC, eight hours of sleep passed in an instant and reality never stopped. Without dreams, there was no escape. People went insane quickly.

The mass suicides began in August, and before the month

was out there wasn't a country in the world that hadn't been caught in the conflagration. When we weren't killing ourselves, we were killing each other. Simmering geo-political tensions erupted into all-out wars, already violent conflicts spiraled out of control, and civilian atrocities became a way of life. Three months after OC, itchy trigger fingers punched buttons and mushroom clouds blossomed on two continents. The world was gripped by terror and madness and six months after OC the global death toll reached five million.

The United Nations & Corporate State Organization held an emergency summit in Cairo and vowed to commit the resources of the world to solving the problem. Oneirologists likened it to Colony Collapse Disorder, the phenomenon that wiped out bee populations earlier in the century and left the global food supply teetering on the brink of disaster. Then synth-feed was developed and seeded in all available farmland, and while our diet has never been more monotonous at least it is reliable. They found a way to synthesize crops and eight months after OC they found a way to synthesize dreams. The Mahindra Corporation, a cyber-prosthetic manufacturer in India, announced the creation of Oneiric Simulation Sub-Cranial Devices, soon known colloquially as Dream Catchers.

After the first wave of DC implantation-trials, the world waited breathlessly for the reports. When it was announced that the trials had been a success and that dreams had been resurrected, newsfeeds showed global celebrations that lasted for weeks. According to the UNCSO Manama Accord, every person on earth was due a Dream Catcher and before the year was out every human on earth had a DC jacked into their skull.

"I think I'll head down to Utopia today," I say after I swallow the last of my synth-bacon.

Mei looks up at me and I feel ashamed by the mild surprise in her eyes.

"I know it's been too long."

"It's good you're going. He'll be happy to see you."

"What will you do while I'm gone? Paint?" I ask hopefully.

Mei laughs as if I've made a joke and flicks on her tablet, aiming it at the wall. As her favorite re-run begins to play, I feel myself mouthing the words of the punch lines, like a dreamspool I have seen too many times.

For a second I consider telling her everything, like I have almost every morning for the past year. I've been seeing Guman's face in my dreams, I imagine saying. And my dreams…are different. I imagine the disbelief that would play across her face, before finally giving way to panic, or as close to panic as anyone can get these days. I know Mei would rush me to a med-tech office and demand an emergency DC replacement. I also know that wouldn't help; even when DC's malfunction, they never malfunction like this.

I bend to kiss the top of her soft blonde curls. I want to say I miss you, but I settle for goodbye.

After they announced the creation of DCs, everyone on earth was categorized to determine when they would be eligible for implantation. I was rated an R12 - non-essential sector employee, over 18, no dependents. My rating gave me an estimated wait time of 5 months before implantation and I used that time to pore over DC schematics and all the literature I could find hoping I would stay sane long enough to get my own.

Dream Catchers are beautiful - cortical wires, neocortex ports, prefrontal dampers, dream sequence filaments, the gear spirals like a galaxy in the liminal space between the brain and the skull. The spiral is an ancient shape, one that our ancestors painted on cave walls and burned onto the sides of grassy hills, and now we have woven it out of manmade fibers and laced it onto our brains.

At the bottom of the stairwell leading outside I pause and take deep swallows of air to quiet my churning stomach. Every time I go out it is getting worse. I push open the door and step into the hot winds whipping into Darwin from the Timor Sea. As I get closer to the bus depot I am swallowed by a crowd of pedestrians and we bump and jostle against one another like a school of fish, oblivious and silent. I tell myself it's irrational, but I feel like I'm walking through a movie set and I'm the only person who knows we're all actors. I lower my head against the wind and hurry.

At the depot I purchase a ticket for Utopia and realize with a flush of shame that it has been almost three years since I have visited my grandfather. When I was a kid, after my parents died, I was moved into a foster home north of the city. Guman visited me every month, which meant he had to beg rides from friends, barter with long-haul truckers, and walk miles in both directions. But as a kid, all I knew was that my favorite person was coming to see me and I waited beneath the eucalyptus tree in the front yard, dying for the first glimpse of his flat brimmed hat and glowing smile as he crested the rise in the road.

That first year, when all I could do was ache for my parents, I spent most of Guman's visits in his arms crying. He always held me patiently, until he could coax a smile from me with one of the treasures he brought in his leather satchel. Sometimes it was tiny seashells or strangely shaped pebbles, but most often it was what I loved best of all, little red sweetberries. They were real, not synth-feed imitations, and they were so tart they made my toes curl. I would eat berry after berry, staining my fingers and lips, content to listen in silence while Guman sang.

He began singing to me from his first visit, songs that were as strong and pure as fresh water in the desert. Eventually, he taught me the words, the melodies and, finally, the meanings.

"These aren't just songs," he said one evening, as lightning bugs flashed lazy messages along the edge of the yard. "These are songlines and they're the maps of the Yonglu." He poked a finger at my chest and then at his own. "That's us, my kid."

I laughed, thinking he was teasing me as he often did, and my mouth felt slow and sticky with sweetberry juice. "How can a song be a map?"

"When you listen to the words and they tell you where to go, that's how," Guman explained. "If you know your land, the songs can take you anywhere you need. The words can even guide you over great distances. If we sing these songs, my kid, we remember who we are and we are never lost."

I find an empty seat in the depot's cavernous waiting room, drop my bag to my feet, and scan the screens that cover every surface. They are flashing decade old re-runs peppered with advertisements for programs and films that never came out. The only new footage these days are the newsfeeds, which are mainly just weather reports highlighting the extreme climatic events that have become commonplace. The screen closest to me is showing a report on the North American brown bear. After years of relentless drought and heat waves, the species has finally succumbed to extinction, joining their arctic brethren who disappeared three decades ago.

None of the people watching this particular screen make a sound. Some yawn and look away. Others drift toward the café-machines, to deliberate between one type of reconstituted synth-meal and another.

After the world was jacked, this unexpected phenomenon, soon known as the Stabilizing Effect, moved across our minds like a low-pressure weather system. Weeks after global implantation, things went silent. People don't talk much anymore, birthrates have fallen, and, most remarkably, a blanket of peace has descended over the world. Decades old wars, the most brutal conflicts, all evaporated. There were no peace summits or iron-clad treaties, people simply drifted away from the front lines, losing interest and vehemence in equal measure.

At first, we were so overjoyed with this new age of Pax Universalis that we didn't notice the other results of The Stabilizing Effect; we listen to old music, watch old films, and read the same books over and over again, because nothing new is ever produced. Art is now viewed with a curious detachment, like a vaguely interesting relic from a bygone era. DCs have slashed and burned the unpredictable vegetation of our psyches to the ground and seeded our mindscapes with synthetic dreams that sprout in orderly, regimented fashion. The great dark forest inside our souls has been turned into farmland, and life carries on.

Mei and I met just before the OC at one of her gallery openings. This blonde creature rushed up to my friends and me as soon as we entered the gallery, all kinetic smile and bawdy laugh, and I think I was in love by the time she introduced herself. She moved in with me soon after and filled the corner of our bedroom with canvases and a forest of spiky paintbrushes and I used to spend evenings in bed, a devout audience of one, watching her paint as the light seeped from the sky.

After OC, Mei stopped painting and she never seemed to mind. Neither did I. Not until this year.

There is movement at one end of the depot and I see the bus to Utopia has arrived. I file onto the carriage, surrounded by the vacant faces of my fellow passengers. I'm trying not to think too far ahead, I don't want to lose the momentum it has taken nearly a year for me to gain. I feel like a child running to their parent, blindly trusting that somehow they will make everything better.

For years my DC worked perfectly. My dreams were reliable and banal. I sat on the moonlit beach, I watched the mountain sunset, and I laughed with faceless friends that didn't exist in my waking life. The dreamspools always worked, until one night they didn't. I don't mean they bounced or shorted or fragged, nothing like that. Those were standard deviations and easily fixed. This was unlike anything I'd ever heard about.

It was the moonlit beach. I was always happy when this spool came up because the rendering was not half bad. The yellow moon hung overhead in an indigo sky and I sat watching the gentle waves; it was all unfolding exactly as it always did.

Until I wasn't alone anymore. At first I just sensed a presence, so I got up and began walking along the beach, pushing the parameters of allowable experience until the dream buffeted me backward. In old-style dream logic I realized the figure was to my right, in the foliage flanking the shore, the face barely noticeable, darker than the shadows and utterly still.

"Guman?" I asked, as the dream fragged and I woke up.

The next day, I went to a med-tech office and explained the vision to the doctor.

"A face? In the moonlit beach spool?" The doctor, a pale man with peach fuzz on his upper lip, looked baffled. "Did you buy a knock-off 'spool, maybe? They can be dangerous, you know, fungal blooms, frayed circuits."

I shook my head. "This wasn't a knock-off. Government issue spool 43A."

He checked my gear, praising the cleanliness of my ducts as he keyed in the diagnostic code to my display panel.

"Everything seems to be in working order, Mx. Arrolealis. I wouldn't be too concerned if I were you." He smiled at me like I was a naughty child. "I suspect what you experienced was just a particularly vivid day-dream. A simple case of imagination run amok." He closed my file on his tablet and opened the door, ready for the next patient.

Once Guman appeared, everything else about my dreams began to change, too. Even when he wasn't present, there were constant deviations from the script I'd dreamed for the past eight years. The ocean in the moonlit beach was choppy with rough waves. The walk through the peaceful park was a torment of mud and hail. The laughter with friends spool became crying, and then kissing, and then a frenzy of faceless sex. When I woke from that one, I reached for Mei, unable to remember the last time I'd felt such urgency. After that, the spools unwound completely, and I was adrift in pure wild-dream for the first time in almost a decade. It was like being in free-fall in my own subconscious and I never wanted it to end.

But it did, every morning, when I woke up to find that nothing else had changed. The world shuffled on beneath its synthetic caul and I wondered if I was going crazy.

I tried to talk about it with Mei, my voice stumbling to explain the feeling that I'd woken up and noticed the sun for the first time. She was confused and then worried. She told me I was making her tired and she needed to sleep. When she woke up she never mentioned it again so neither did I.

I ride the bus for 23 hours, first through the endless stretch of suburbs that ring Darwin, then through a vastness of empty countryside. Red clouds of dust billow from the side of the road and I watch them dissipate into the bleached bone sky until it stains my vision orange. It hasn't rained here in months, and isn't expected to anytime soon.

It was another consequence of the Stabilizing Effect, an unintended side-effect of an unintended side-effect. In the years immediately preceding the OC, the world had started to address what had long been considered a lost cause and great strides were finally made to avert the impending eco-cide. CO2 levels were brought down, critically endangered ecosystems were coaxed into equilibrium, and the people of Beijing, Bombay, and Los Angeles, saw stars for the first time in decades.

On my last visit to Guman before the OC, we were sitting outside his little house, admiring the wild tangle of his non-synth vegetable garden, planted with exceedingly rare wild seeds, and discussing the announcement we had just seen on the newsfeed. The Great Barrier Reef, long thought to be a completely dead 2,300-kilometer testament to humankind's failure, was exhibiting signs of life. Great green swathes of Porites coral surrounded by clouds of fish had been spotted, news of which startled experts and fed the growing hope shared by the rest of us; perhaps we hadn't doomed the planet, after all.

"I didn't think I'd live to see this day, my kid," Guman said, plucking a bright red sweetberry from the plant at his feet and popping it into his mouth. "It just goes to show you, there's always hope."

But after global DC implantation, that budding impetus shriveled and died, unrealized and incomplete. We turned away from the fight, all of us. We watched the reports that came more frequently over the years, as the carbon emissions once again soared, as rising seawaters gradually submerged coastlines, and as ecosystems collapsed one after the other. We watch the reports, we nod to one another, and we turn away to hide in manufactured fantasy while the world burns.

I know of precisely one human being that isn't hiding in synth dreams, one human that was never implanted; Guman. I visited him soon after my implantation, when it first started to seem like humanity might actually survive the OC. I'd been geared up for six weeks and was still swimming through a cloud of giddy relief. Guman met me on the tarmac of the bus depot, where he pulled me down for a kiss and then looked up at the fading pink scar beneath my left ear.

"Ah, my kid. Full-on cyborg now, yeah?"

I laughed incredulously. "Of course. Like every other human being."

He gave me a wink and lifted the brim of his flat-billed hat to expose the DC-free peppercorn curls behind his left ear.

I was stunned. "Guman, hasn't your number come up? They said everyone in the NT had been implanted. Why didn't you tell me you needed help getting registered?"

He waved me away and turned to begin the walk to his house, but I pressed on, horrified.

"We need to go right now to a med-tech office, this is unacceptable," I said, hurrying after him. "We have to make a complaint. You should have had a DC by now!" I was furious for a few more moments until I realized he was smiling.

I stopped and let him walk on as the realization washed over me. "You didn't register, did you? Guman, why? What are you thinking?"

"I'm thinking," he began, as I caught up to him, "that I couldn't handle having a computer for a brain."

Words tumbled out of me in disarray. "It's not like that, it's a relief. Your dreams come back. Aren't you going mad without them?"

"No more than I was before," he answered with a laugh.

A disorienting sense of unease unwound in my chest as I imagined life without a DC, remembering the dark, endless months before I was implanted. "You can't do this, Guman. People can't survive without gear."

Guman didn't respond and we walked on into the setting sun. I struggle now to recall any other memories from that visit, it is all clouded over by the horror of what Guman had done.

I used to visit him several times a year, but since that first post-DC visit 9 years ago, I have only gone to see him twice. Guman never got a rig; he was the only person I heard of to have survived without implantation, and the thought of his life of seamless awake was simply too much for me. I eventually stopped visiting him, I tried to not even think about him, until he appeared in my dreams and unraveled my world.

When I disembark at the Utopia depot, night has fallen. I turn off the main road and head down the hard packed dirt path toward Guman's house. He has no tablet so I haven't been able to let him know I am visiting and I hope I will find him at home. I end up finding him outside, where he is sitting on a wooden bench next to his front door and I almost don't see him from behind the tall twists of plants in his garden.

He stands up slowly and I am silenced by the sight of him. Guman has been old as long as I've known him, but now he is ancient and withered, a small pillar of a person, like a des- iccated termite mound baked frail in the heat. But his smile still glows like the rising sun and he puts his hands to my face and kisses me. "My kid, my kid, it is good to see you."

He holds me close for a long moment as I begin to cry. Anyone else in the world would be astonished to see my tears, but not Guman, and they flow without comment. Long minutes pass before he leans back, wipes the tears from my cheek and takes me by the hand. We turn away from his house and the dim lights of town, and begin walking into the bush. As my eyes adjust to the darkness, fat baobab trees melt out of the shadows and we drop into a dry riverbed, turning to follow its winding track.

We walk for a time in silence and I let the darkness soothe

the ache in my throat until I trust myself to speak. "Guman, I'm sorry. I'm sorry I stayed gone for so long."

"No apologies needed, my kid."

"It was wrong," I say to his back. "I can't believe I let so much time pass."

Guman waves a hand over his shoulder. "I told you, no apologies needed. You were having a hard time, you did what you needed to do."

In the distance I hear the swirling cry of the willarroo, something I haven't heard since I was a child. The stars shimmer overhead and make the night sky feel very close and very large, all at once. I can hear Guman breathing ahead of me and I feel safe.

"I've missed you, Guman."

He glances back at me over his shoulder, "Missed me? Haven't we seen each other almost every night, my kid?"

He reaches out and takes my hand and we walk on together in silence. The night hangs like a mantel of velvet from the stars overhead, and as the moon climbs higher in the sky, following its own path through the night, Guman begins to sing.

"I Rise up and begin

Begin with the earth

Flat trail of sun under my feet

I Rise up and begin"

I look down and see that Guman has led us onto a rust-red wrinkle of earth that glows like a dim sun in the darkness and winds like a subterranean snake. He continues singing and his voice is as deep and wide as ocean current, filling the night with his words.

It is a songline, one Guman taught me so many years ago.
And it is, of course, the path we are following.

"Waves of land, moving stone

I walk on the water of the earth

I swim on the waves of the earth"

The path we are on begins to change, small hummocks of
earth bubble beneath our feet, miniature peaks and valleys,
and we roll over them like earthbound ships.

"We walk through the valleys of darkness and day

We dream ourselves awake"

Guman looks back at me, and for a single disorienting
moment I think I can feel the earth spin on its axis beneath
my feet. The faint smell of wood-smoke, salt, and honey
fill the air, and somehow I know we have entered Guman's
dreamscape. I wait for this to feel strange or impossible, but
the feeling never comes.

"The path grows dark

We meet ourselves now

We rise up and begin"

Awareness. A figure stands to our right. Guman and I stop
and turn to face the shadow among shadows, a man alone in
a vast landscape. It is Guman, another Guman, surrounded
by a forest that is as tall as it is wide; it circles the earth and
is filled with all creation. A shadow moves across the sky
and darkness falls over the forest, which I now realize is the
dreamscape, the wild-dreams of all humanity. The shadow
eats away at the trees, ripping the foliage from branches, and
Guman watches while the dreamscape is devoured, receding
in all directions, before fading into the distance and vanish-
ing entirely. He is now an island, exposed and adrift in a
lifeless seabed. I turn to face the Guman standing next to me
and I see he has already begun walking on.

"I cross water first

I cross water again

I rise up and begin"

I smell water, clear as daylight in the dry air. We cross a stream and then another and our feet carry halos of moisture into the dry dirt of the path.

Guman stops in front of me and raises an arm, pointing through the darkness to a figure standing in a grove of thorn trees. It is Guman again and he is walking, following a trail, searching for something, waiting for it to speak to him. I begin to understand he is tracking his lost dreams through the wasteland of his own mind, following memories so faint they are nothing more than spores carried on the wind.

This Guman kneels and begins to dig in the dusty earth. Then, he lifts something from the ground and holds it up to the moonlight where it catches the light like a pearl before he places it reverently into his satchel. Dreamseed.

I see Guman walking his dreamscape for years, the only person awake in a world of artificial dreams, on a quest for something no one remembers. His bent figure shuffles through the wasteland, waiting months and even years between each discovery. With a tremor of agony, I realize that Guman never planted a single dreamseed for himself; he never again dreamed. He hoarded the seeds, sacrificing his own mind to shield them from the darkness.

I turn to the Guman standing next to me and he opens the satchel at his hip. I peer inside and begin to cry; his seed vault, his great collection, is so small, there are so few. He lifts the satchel over his head and hands it to me. Wordlessly, I place it around my neck and feel it fall to my hip, where the dreamseeds rustle softly in their dark womb.

"I planted one in you, last year," he says. "And one was all it took. Some may need more. You'll learn how to judge soon enough, my kid."

He turns and we walk on, singing together now.

"The earth brings me to shelter

Together we begin."

The path leads us beneath the overhanging lip of a gorge, and as we walk, I catch the faint smell of sweetberries in the air, and salt water, and, faint as a sigh, the acrid tang of Mei's paint; we have crossed into my dreamscape and I am singing louder now. Guman's voice has fallen to a whisper, but I know the song, he taught me well and I can sing for us both.

We come to a thick grove of wild vegetation and I know it is where Guman planted that first dreamseed in my mind. I recognize the plant that sprouted from that seed, standing tall and gnarled in the center of the copse, while other plants radiate out from it in a gentle spiral shape. From that one seed, these plants have grown and I move through them slowly, collecting as many seeds as I can find.

I can see Guman's plan unfolding on the horizon and taking shape against the night sky. He intends for me to use these dreamseeds to rewild humankind's mind and I feel humbled and exhilarated and mad with hope. I think of what this will mean to the world, the return of passion, of art, of laughter, of one last chance to save the planet and ourselves.

Then I feel a rough current of fear as I think of resurrecting not just wild-dreams, but also what we have come to know as their dark siblings, violence, pain, and war. I turn back to Guman and he looks at me for a long moment, his tired eyes intent on my own, until the fear ebbs and only its echo remains as a warning. I know I will plant these seeds and I know I will share these songs, these paths, this knowing, this dreaming. They are all intertwined and the one is inseparable from the other. It is time for us to become fully human, earth-animals dreaming ourselves awake.

I turn and lead the way up the gorge. Guman has stopped singing but I am not afraid because I know this song and I know where it leads.

"I rise up and begin

Awake with dreaming

I climb through the night until dawn

I rise up and begin"

When I wake, I'm standing at the top of the gorge, watching the sunrise melt the blue shadows on the rock, my satchel of dreamseeds hanging at my side. I am alone and I know I won't see Guman again. I turn and begin the walk back to Utopia, to the bus depot, Darwin, and home.

***

I began with Mei. For weeks, I sang myself into her dreams and waited in spool after spool, mountain sunset, moonlit beach, steak and mash, waiting for her to notice me. It started with a look, confusion in her dark eyes. She approached my figure as I crouched in the foliage of the moonlit beach and reached for me. I let her feel what I was feeling; I helped her dream what I was dreaming, and to my surprise she accepted immediately. We planted a dreamseed into the soil of her dreamscape, singing together, slowly at first as I taught her the words and then with full-throated shouts of joy. It took her mind several tries to shrug off the DC's hold, but when it did, when she was free, it was spectacular. The thorny undergrowth that had slept dormant for so long leapt forth in a great quaking explosion; it was beauty and pain all at once.

And then we reveled, running through her dreams like children let out after too long inside. We climbed trees in the peaceful park, skinning our knees bloody on their rough bark. We chased each other, tumbling like laughing goats down the scree of the sunset mountains. We moved together as one on the shore of the moonlit beach, urgent ecstasy beneath indigo sky. And then we left the dreamspools entirely and spiraled through her wild-dreams, lost and awake and rejoicing. Like the art she made that first morning after waking from a wild-dream filled sleep; it was vivid, textured, and vulgar, thick red paint dripping off taut canvas. It was a terrible, human kind of beauty.

THE SAVE

Nicole Robb

There are two things in the world that I truly love: Writing and travel.

When I'm not jotting down memoirs of my adventures around the world, I'm often scribbling down fantasy or sci-fi short stories to serve as vehicles to convey my pride, frustration, confusion, or random "what if" thoughts about what's going on in the world around me.

I've recently completed my first novel, "Children of the Midnight Sun", with the hopes of finding a publisher in the near future.

It's almost midnight when I arrive home. I stand on our porch and grope the inner lining of my purse for my keys. Behind the living room curtains, I see the faint flicker of coloured lights from the television.Dad's waiting up for me.

I slip inside the house and tip-toe towards my room. I haven't broken curfew, but I am guilty of consuming a few under-age drinks. Not many tonight—only two. Enough to make me socially acceptable to my friends without fear of being a colossal disappointment to my father should he catch me.I glance inside the living room as I walk past it, hoping to avoid his comments about the length of my skirt or the colour of my lipstick. For a moment, I think he's already asleep, but he isn't. He's slouched in the corner of the couch, staring ahead at the television screen.

I'm busted.

"Hey, Dad." He doesn't respond. He doesn't even grunt to indicate his disapproval of my late night socializing.

Had I not been drinking, perhaps I would have realized it in four steps. Or three. But instead, I take five full steps towards my bedroom before I stop and turn. Something is wrong. I back up to the living room entrance and peer inside. My father is motionless. His eyes are half open and unfocused. He looks much paler than usual.

"Dad?"

No answer.

I run to his side and put my hand on his shoulder. His left arm is twisted and tightly clenched. My stomach tightens.

I shake him. Nothing.

"Daddy?"

No answer.

I slap him. Hard. His head droops forward like a broken puppet. Nothing.

"Daddy!" A heavy sob escapes my mouth like a volcano erupting from the back of my throat. My fingers frantically probe the sides of his throat for a pulse. I have no more words to plead with, only mangled sounds squeezing past the tightness in my throat. But I don't let myself cry. I have a job to do. I have one chance at this.

My one Save.

In elementary school, they made us practice Saves on a dummy. I remember the boys in my class laughing when they were instructed to spread their hands over a dummy with a blossomed chest. The following year, the school switched to gender neutral dolls. Mary-Ann Tenner, my classmate, sat in the corner of the room and did math problems while we practiced. She had accidentally Saved her cat when she was four years old. Apparently she had found it under her bed, lifeless, and cuddled with it until it suddenly sprang to life in her arms. She said her mother scolded her for wasting her Save and wouldn't let her play outside for three days. Of course, Mary-Ann didn't even know what a Save was until she started school.

You can only Save once, the teachers used to tell us. *Make sure it's for the right reason.* The more conservative teachers warned us that Saved people never come back quite as they originally were. They said everyone loses a part of themselves when they die—a part that can never be replaced. The religious nuts even told us that all children were granted Saves as a test from God, and that using our Save meant we failed, or conformed, or some other bullshit.

His body feels stiff. His hands are clutched into fists, and his twisted arm is unnaturally rigid as I struggle to move him into a more accessible position on the couch. At school, we were taught that these are common signs of a heart attack. His half-open eyes distract me, and I run my fingers softly over his eyelids to close them. I think of my mother. I always assumed my Save would be used on her. She is alone, in a hospital bed only a few blocks away. The doctors say she's comfortable, that it could be days, or weeks, or months before she goes. Suddenly, I feel more torn than I ever thought possible.

We've never talked about who I would use my Save on. I've tried to bring it up with my parents a few times, discreetly, but they refuse to discuss it. My parents, the perfect law abiding citizens. I always found it interesting that only teachers are allowed to talk to us minors about Saves. Punishment is strict for anyone, especially our own parents, who bring up the subject with us prior to our Save being used. When we were six, Leanne Wilson's father went to jail for forcing her to Save her sister after a car accident. In History class we learn about the days when children were sold, or kidnapped, for their Saves. Some parents even forced their children to Save before their third birthday, just to protect them from grieving maniacs who would do anything to get their loved ones back. At the time, I could understand the need for the strictness of the *Save Bill*. I even wrote an essay on it.

But, right now, I think it's the stupidest goddamn law ever written.

Mom knows she's going to die. She's prepared, but was Dad?

The other side of my brain plays Devil's Advocate. *Your mom gave birth to you. She cooked and cleaned and taught you how to read. Your dad smoked and ate like shit. She deserves a second chance more than he does.* Then, the nagging bitch in the very centre of my brain—the same one who makes me second guess myself during exams—slams me with one final question. *It's very simple, Janice. Who do you love more?*

I need a few minutes to think. I know I have some time, but not much. I aced the test on Save Time Limits back in grade school: we have a maximum of ten hours to Save heart attack casualties. I kneel beside the couch and stare down at my father. The tears come. I let them flow. They land on his chest, forming wet blotches on his shaggy blue housecoat. I search his eyes for any sign of direction. Did he want to be Saved? His face looks peaceful. Was his death quick? Did he know it was coming? I take a few deep breaths and notice the cordless phone on the floor in front of the couch. *He was trying to call for help! He didn't want to die!* I stand and place the phone in its cradle on the coffee table, beside the remote controls and Dollar Store notepad. I see the note I had left for him that afternoon: *Dad, I've gone to visit Mom and then out with some friends. Home by midnight.* Love ya.

Love ya. It's as simple as that. But above all, I need him.

I open his robe, place my hands over his chest. The positioning is easy after rehearsing it so many times in school. My thumbs each rest on either side of his breastbone. The tips of my fingers spread above each of his nipples, as if I'm cradling his lungs and heart. I close my eyes and feel a warmth in my fingertips.

"Come back," I say. It's that simple.

Before I even open my eyes, I feel his chest rise as he takes a deep breath. I look at him. His eyes aren't open yet, but his colouring has returned to normal. There's even a red mark on his cheek where I slapped him. I remove my hands and sit on the floor. I watch, and I wait.

One breath. Two breaths. On his third breath his eyes open. He blinks a few times before he notices me.

"Janice." His voice is soft and hoarse.

"It's okay, Dad. I Saved you."

"I was having a heart attack, I think. But..." he looks around the room. At the TV, at the floor, at the side table, at his left arm, and then at me. I smile. The tears flow down my face. My lower lip quivers and my cheeks feel flushed. I lean forward, wrap my arms around him, and sob with my head on his chest for what feels like hours. He strokes my hair with his right hand.

"I love you so much, Dad."

"I love you too, Kiddo."

I back away as he lifts himself into a seated position. His eyes are distant, like he's focusing on the dust particles somewhere in the space between me and the television.

"Are you all right?"

"I'm fine, Kiddo. But, apparently being Saved takes a lot out of a person. I'm exhausted."

"Maybe I should sleep in the same room as you? Just to make sure you're okay." We both know he will sleep in the living room. He hasn't slept in his bed since my mother was admitted to the hospital. "I'll just grab my sleeping bag and stay right here." I point to the floor.

"Sure. If it will make you feel better."

I start to walk away, but he calls my name. I turn and look at him from the hallway. He takes a breath before continuing.

"Thank you."

I smile.

As I rummage through my closet for my sleeping bag, I hear my father enter the kitchen and run the sink. He opens and shuts cupboards, grabs something from the fridge, and then walks towards the bathroom. He seems to be acting normal, and for that I am grateful. I've heard horror stories of Saved people who came back angry, or worse, with no memory of the person who Saved them.

I return to the living room, unroll my sleeping bag on the floor and turn off the television and lights. My father settles himself back onto the couch and wishes me goodnight.

"Janice?" he says, his voice a sleepy whisper in the darkness.

"Yeah?"

"You're a good daughter." Within seconds, he's snoring.

I close my eyes but my brain isn't letting me sleep. My mind is racing. I wonder about my mother, about how I'll feel when she dies and there's nothing I can do about it. *It's an even bigger decision than sex*, some of the teachers used to tell us. True, it was a big decision, but I don't regret it. I hear my father snoring peacefully beside me. My mind flashes to the image of him dead on the couch. His body slouched in an unnatural position. His lifeless eyes, his twisted arm, his clenched fist...

My eyes pop open. That nagging bitch inside my head compels me to stand and walk to the kitchen. I had heard my father opening cupboards a few minutes ago. The cupboard under the sink, where the garbage bin is located, always makes a distinctive creak when it's opened quickly. I pause, make sure he's still snoring, and pull the garbage bin out of the cupboard. I don't have to search long. The crumpled piece of paper is still in a ball on top of the used paper towels and empty milk cartons.

My hands shake as they unfold the paper. I know exactly where it came from. I realize now, after Saving him, that I never saw him un-clench his left fist. I instantly recognize the Dollar Store note paper from our coffee table. It has only one word written on it. The message I was supposed to find.

DON'T.

FEEDING IS NO CRIME

Patricia Russo

"If, as it is stated in the Code of Padrel the Great, that eating is no crime, then it follows by corollary that neither is feeding a criminal offense."

Six months of law school, and that was the way Zerna talked now? It rubbed Fonell the wrong way, like she was trying to show off. Come on, his friend Drau said. She's learned some new words. What do you expect happens when you go to school? She's still the same Zerna now that she's always been.

She didn't dress the same. Fonell didn't figure scholarships covered trips to upmarket boutiques. A boyfriend?

A boyfriend would have given her jewelry, dumbass, Drau said. She probably got a job on campus and bought herself a couple of nice things. Big deal. Anyway, I don't know why you're getting your nutsack in a twist for. You two broke up before Zerna went away.

Fonell punched Drau in the arm. We were never together, asshole, he said. But she could've dressed down for a visit to the old neighborhood.

Especially when the visit was more in the nature of an emergency call.

"Is that all you have to say?" shouted someone who lived in the building behind which some kids had found the white strip in the dirt where the paving had been torn up and some earth removed to get to a sewage line that turned out not to be there. Of course they ran and told other kids, and a great swarm of youngsters had dug for hours, thinking they were going to find buried treasure, before some adult with a bit of brains had remembered what that shiny, white, plasticky-metallic-magical material had been used by the old emperors for, what they'd intended to seal up tight and forever.

A thousand years had passed since the time of the old emperors, and forever was apparently not as long as the emperors or their magicians had thought. The kids had managed not only to produce a truly impressive excavation, but also to break one edge of the white sealant and reveal the pit below it.

A thousand years, and the prisoners were still alive.

Damn the old emperors and damn their magicians, Fonell thought as he looked at Zerna, standing there in her nice boots and dove-gray cloak. Maybe he shouldn't have called her. She looked a little sick, and she was standing way back from the pit.

Everybody could hear the prisoners' cries. A thousand years, and languages changed as well as governments and systems of magic, the new superseding the old, but echoes remained. The word for food was not the same now as it had been in the time of the old emperors, but it was close enough that old canny Canly figured it out within minutes. Food, the people, or former people, in the pit called for, over and over. Only food, not water. Fonell found that strange. He also thought it was odd that no stench came from the pit. No smell at all, in fact.

Canly had argued from the start that they should put all the dirt back, bury the pit, and pave it over.

"And forget about them?" Drau had asked. "You can listen to that," he pointed at the pit, "and say forget it?"

"We can't help them."

"The seal's been broken. We could get them out."

A neighborhood meeting, it was, held out in the open and on the spot in question, so that later nobody could say anything had been kept secret or any dealings had been done behind anybody else's back. That was the tradition of their neighborhood.

Canly shouted, "Do you really think that would be a kindness? A thousand years or more, trapped in undying bodies—undying, hungering bodies. And I bet you anything that it is impossible for them to eat. Cruel bastards, those old emperors."

"We don't know if they can eat or not," Vamma, who was almost as old as Canly, said. "We don't know anything. What's the law on this? Does this count as an archeological find?"

As soon as Vamma said 'law', most of the crowd groaned. That was the most ancient tradition of all—never involve the authorities. But then Vamma's mother had married into the neighborhood, so she wasn't really quite one of them.

The only time you saw municipal guards on these streets was when they were escorting an ambulance or a fire brigade—and it had to be one hell of an emergency for someone in the neighborhood to call for outside assistance. They were people who took care of each other; they had their own doctors, their own curers and menders, and if anyone called out, "Fire!" there'd be two dozen men and women converging with buckets and hoses to put it out faster than a bird could shit.

Vamma flapped her hands at the groaners. "The government should decide what to do. This is too big for just us to take responsibility for."

"No, it isn't," Onjar, who ran the laundry down the block

and a café outside of the neighborhood and a few other things besides. "It's big, but it's here. It's here, so it's ours. You want to call the bloody government in? What'll they do? Cordon off the area, obstruct the streets, and disrupt our lives for months while they dither. Be serious."

"They might know how to help."

"There is no help," Canly insisted.

"We have scientists as well as magicians now, you know," Vamma said.

"And every single one of them will come to the same conclusion—after months of debating and dithering, like Onjar said. Let's just get it over with now."

"I'm sure there are laws about this."

"And I'm sure you're right. There are laws about everything."

That got a smattering of laughs.

Vamma glared. "I think it would be nice to know what the laws are before we start breaking them willy-nilly."

And Fonell, because the idea of burying the crying people made his stomach hurt, spoke up. "I know a lawyer. She can give us her legal opinion."

Naturally everyone gathered around the pit understood he was talking about Zerna. They also knew that she had only just started law school and wasn't actually a lawyer, and that she and Fonell used to see each other. However—a fact which carried great weight—they knew that Zerna was from an old neighborhood family, so even though she'd chosen to go to school in some snooty place all the way at the other end of the province, she could be trusted. Canly grumbled that it was a waste of time, but he went along with the suggestion to contact her.

Now here she was, standing too far from the pit, talking about the Code of Padrel the Great.

"Padrel the Great was a long time ago," some idiot who didn't even live on the block said.

"His Code still forms the foundation of our modern common law," Zerna said.

Drau said, "That's good to know. Zerna, we're all glad you came."

Asshole, Fonell thought, though he knew Drau was only trying to smooth things over.

Zerna hadn't answered the phone the first couple of times Fonell had tried to call. When he finally heard a live Hello, he immediately said, "This is neighborhood business. Can we talk?"

"Let me call you back," she said, and a few minutes later she had, from somewhere, Fonell assumed, more private. He'd explained, briefly, what the kids had found, and how the neighborhood folks weren't sure what they should do.

"I'll be there tomorrow," she said, and hung up before Fonell could say, It's good to hear your voice.

Despite that, on the phone she'd sounded like herself. Sharp, confident, and catching on quick. The old Zerna, the one whose brain would get her out of the neighborhood, but whose heart would bring her back.

She seemed so different now. It wasn't just the clothes, or the way she'd braided her hair. Her demeanor was…off. She'd arrived on the train, but hadn't alerted anyone to meet her, and she hadn't brought any luggage. She'd come to the site on her own, on foot, and waited until the grapevine rustled up a crowd, which included Canly and Vamma, but no member of her own family. It had taken Fonell a while to realize that. Her parents were dead, but she had a buttload of aunts and uncles and several buttloads of cousins, and not one of them was here.

And she was looking ill, as if she didn't want to be here herself.

"They want to be fed," she said.

"We know that," Canly said. He'd been standing back, but now he pushed forward. "And I say, as I've said from the beginning, that there's nothing we can do to help them. They can't be human anymore, not after all this time. There are no people in that pit, only appetites."

Immediately, Vamma cut in. "What I want to know is the law about archeological finds. We're supposed to report them, aren't we? All antiquities belong to the state."

"Do you expect to get a reward?" Canly sneered. "Do you hear this, Zerna? You hear this nonsense? Archeology and antiquities, for pity's sake."

"Pity," Zerna said. She swayed a little, in her polished, high-heeled boots. "How many of them are there? Have you looked?"

Onjar, the businessman, said, "We sent someone down with a rope around his waist and a flashlight. He couldn't see much. The kids broke the seal, but the opening isn't much wider than your little finger. He said he saw figures, and he thought he saw eyes, reflecting the light from the flashlight, but not much else."

"She's shaking," Drau whispered in Fonell's ear. "Why is she shaking?"

"I don't know."

"None of her family is here. Did you notice?"

"Yes. Shut up."

Old neighborhood family. Old lineage. How old?

A thousand years ago or more, what sort of place had this been? After the fall of the emperors, there had been much destruction, heaping loads of chaos. People fleeing in one direction, other people fleeing the opposite way. But some people always stayed put, didn't they? Hunkered down and rode things out?

Until the kids had uncovered the punishment vault, Fonell would have sworn that no remnant of that ancient period remained anywhere in the neighborhood. Not a building stone, not a shard of pottery, not a dirt-encrusted bead from some high-born's headdress. He had never even given a thought to genes.

"Archeological finds and antiquities do not include living beings," Zerna said.

Canly glanced at Vamma with a 'Satisfied, then?' look. "So we bury this mess and that's the end of it. Right?" People were nodding and voicing agreement when Zerna said something. Nobody heard.

She was trembling. She spoke again, and again nobody heard.

Fonell shouted, "Wait! What's wrong with you idiots? Let her talk!"

Canly jerked his head around, then waved for silence. Old canny Canly, his eyes narrowed, but his smile pleasant enough. "Sorry, child. What is it you wanted to say?"

"No."

"What do you mean, no?"

Drau leaned closer to Fonell. "What's going on?"

"I don't know. Shut up." He kept his eyes on Zerna. She was breathing too fast. Something was definitely not right.

"No burying," she said. "We dig more. We break the punishment vault, or pry a bigger hole in it. And we get them out."

The neighborhood folks all started talking at once.

Zerna and Canly stared at each other.

"That is not mercy," Canly said, after the crowd had quieted. "That is cruelty."

"No. Leaving them there is cruelty. They are aware, and they are suffering."

"They are aware only of their suffering, and their suffering will not be eased by releasing them. They will continue to suffer, and we will have to suffer with them. We can already hear them. How much worse will it be when we can see them, too? That is the cruelty I meant."

Vamma stuck her oar in. "Canly, listen. I know we'd have to tend them, take care of them, forever. But like Onjar said, we don't know how many poor creatures are in there. There might be only a few. People–families–could volunteer to take one each. If we bury them again, we're no better than the old emperors and their tame magicians."

Canly shook his head. "And would you volunteer? Volunteer yourself, and your children, and your grandchildren, on and on, generation after generation?"

Drau whispered, "Look at Zerna."

Fonell had never stopped looking at her. She'd put her hands over her face.

Vamma drew herself up. "I do," she said, firmly.

"More fool you," said one of the idiots who didn't live on the block. Canly said nothing.

Zerna dropped her hands. "No."

That No, everybody heard. It was a No of authority. She walked to the edge of the pit and looked down, dread on her face, but also resignation.

To Drau, Fonell said, "You're my best friend. But whatever happens next, stay out of it."

"What are you going to do?"

But Fonell was already walking to the pit. When he stood next to Zerna, she did not glance at him.

The voices were much louder here. Food, food, food. How many different voices? He couldn't tell. Ten? Twenty?

"Vamma," Zerna said. "Your heart is kind. But it's my family that needs to take care of this."

"They're not here," Fonell said. "Not one of them."

"I know," she said. She looked at Canly. "Will you do what I asked? Will you accept my counsel?"

"As long as you accept responsibility."

"I do."

"Zerna, what are you doing?" Fonell asked.

Vamma asked, "Why your family?"

"Because the people inside the punishment vault are our kin."

"I'm sorry I called you," Fonell said. "I should have left you alone."

"You didn't do anything wrong," Zerna said. She looked down into the pit again. "Neither did they. One of them, maybe. But the old emperors punished the entire household for the transgression of one. We've made a lot of progress since then, haven't we? At least we don't do that kind of thing anymore."

"They'll be insane," Canly said. "If they have any minds left at all."

Zerna nodded.

"At best, they'll be…worms in withered human bodies. No more brains than that. I hope so, anyway, for their sake."

"Even worms feel pain," Zerna said. "Are you going to get on with it?"

"Yes. I'll send some people to fetch tools."

"Can you feed them?" Vamma asked.

"I don't know."

"Why isn't anybody from your family here?" Fonell asked. "Are they coming later, when the prisoners are freed?"

"No. Nobody's coming."

She still wasn't looking at him. Fonell saw Drau in the crowd, shaking his head, but Drau didn't understand. He thought Fonell was pining after a lost love or some stupid shit like that.

He and Zerna had never been in love, not romantically. They'd gone to the same day-care center when they were toddlers. They'd played together as children. When they were older, they'd had sex a couple of times, but it had been a casual thing, okay at best, never great, never spectacular.

He'd been delighted for her when she'd been accepted into law school. He'd wanted to celebrate, and she'd come over. Just the two of them, at his place, him pouring wine and burbling about how proud he was, until he finally noticed that she wasn't saying anything, that all the time he'd been bustling around, she'd been sitting on his couch crying.

Her family hadn't approved of her decision to go to law school. She hadn't told any of them that she was applying. When she announced that she'd been admitted, a ruction of epic proportions had erupted. He'd comforted her as best he could, saying that they were ignorant and jealous and backwards, that she had no reason to feel guilty for using her brain. That was the last time they'd been alone together.

Her brain got her out, but it hadn't been her heart that brought her back. It had been him.

"I'm sorry," he said again. "This is my fault."

"No."

"Why won't you look at me?"

He heard her sigh. "This is my responsibility. Go away before you get hurt."

"Leaving you to stay and get hurt?"

"Fonell, please."

"Can we feed them? I know you told Vamma you didn't know, but what do you think? Is it possible?"

After a moment, Zerna said, "I think there is no way of feeding them. But I may be able to comfort them. Hungry and loved is better than hungry and abandoned." She sighed again. "It has to be."

"We may be able to comfort them," Fonell said.

"No. Are you volunteering, too? No. What I told Vamma was true. My family are the only ones who have even a small hope of helping these people. That was woven into the magic that bound them."

"But it doesn't look like your aunts and uncles and cartloads of cousins give a shit about that."

Zerna twitched one shoulder. "They are cowards. I'm glad they cast me out."

"Cast you out?" Fonell hadn't known it had gone that far.

"Informally. Doesn't count legally. Or morally, if it comes to that. Which it does, here."

Drau shouted, "The men with the tools are coming."

"You could still run," Fonell whispered.

"Never."

"I love you," Fonell said, and took her hand. She tried to pull away, but he held on tight. "We both know it. And we both know there are so many different kinds of love. You are going to love these famished, suffering creatures one way. I have loved you since we were both three years old, in another. And you love me…like a puppy. The stupid neighborhood boy with his cute little problems and insignificant life."

"Stop it."

"They're doing what you said. They're coming with tools to break open the punishment vault. And then what? Are you going to comfort all of them? Ten, twenty, however many of poor fuckers have been stuck in there for a thousand years?"

"Yes. It can only be done by family."

"I understand that. But a person can marry into a family."

She turned then, and for the first time in nearly a year, Fonell looked into Zerna's eyes. "No."

"Yes."

"I won't let you. You have a life."

"And you don't? Marry me, Zerna, and we will share what is coming."

"Get away from me."

"No chance. I will hold your hand forever, if that's what it takes. But it won't, will it? I never went to law school–sorry– but I know the government recognizes common-law marriage after three years. So all I have to do is hold your hand for three years. You think I can't manage that?"

"Fonell…"

"Or you could make it easier by saying Yes in front of two witnesses and that old canny Canly."

"Why? You don't need to do this."

"Why? Because I do love you, in one of the seventeen or eighteen thousand ways that love can be defined. We really need more words for this, don't you think? But don't get a big head. It's not only because of you. I was never on Canly's side. Burying them and forgetting them? That's horrible. If there is any way to help, then I want to help. Then my insignificant life might have some significance after all."

"No life is insignificant."

"Right. And that includes the people in the punishment vault."

"My family won't come. I tried calling my great-uncle. He hung up on me."

"I will be your family."

"You don't have to do this."

"Well, neither do you, do you? You didn't even have to get on the train."

Eyes locked, all through the arrival of the men and women with tools, through the expansion of the excavation, the two of them stood, hands clasped.

Canly ordered the diggers about. Vamma approached Fonell and Zerna once, looked at their faces, and retreated.

Drau came to stand just out of arm's reach from them.

Finally, finally, after an eternity (food, food, food coming from the pit, men and women talking and cursing, the sounds of digging and battering and rending) Zerna nodded, once.

"You," Fonell said, pointing at Drau. "And you," he said, pointing at a random woman in the crowd. "Come here. Canly. Over here."

"What is it?" Canly asked.

Drau said, "Fonell, what are you doing?"

The woman said nothing, but came to stand with them.

Fonell said, "Before these two witnesses, under the sky, our hands clasped, Zerna and I will marry."

Canly rolled his eyes. "You're a romantic fool," he said. "And Zerna, you're a bigger one."

"We're making a family," Fonell said.

Canly said, "You're making a mistake, but then there are a lot of mistakes being made today. What's one more?"

"Do it seriously," Zerna said. "You're our binder. Perform the ceremony properly."

"Of course I will. I take it this will be a life-marriage?"

"Yes," Fonell said. Zerna nodded.

"Very well." And as another crew of neighborhood men climbed down into the pit with shovels and crowbars, as Vamma was organizing a group of neighborhood folks to bring a variety of different food items to the site–"We don't know if they can eat. But if they can, they might be able to eat some things and not others. So let's get a little bit of everything we can think of, all right?"–Canly slowly, solemnly, and with impeccable enunciation, recited the words to bind two people in a life-marriage. At the end of it, he even intoned the traditional verse of congratulations. Then he went back to overseeing the diggers in the pit.

"When they come out," Zerna said, "they'll have to be taken somewhere. They won't be able to walk, so they'll need to be carried. Your place, all right?"

"Our place," Fonell said, and that brought a tiny smile to her face.

Food, food, food. The voices were louder now; not even the sounds of digging and of the men swearing as they worked on the crack in the sealant of the punishment vault could muffle them.

"Are you ready for the first one?" Canly called.

Zerna took a deep breath. "Yes."

Naked and withered, contracted into a fetal position, barely moving, except for its mouth, the first prisoner was passed up from the pit. Canly took it. He held it for a moment, looking into its face. "Bring scarves, hats, things like that," he said to Vamma's group. "We'll have to protect their eyes. Light after so long in the dark will be painful."

"My husband can do that," Zerna said.

"What a great start to your honeymoon, boy." Canly laughed softly. How could he laugh while he was holding that contorted, mewling creature that had once been a human being? Fonell thought.

Drau must have read the expression on Fonell's face. He said, "He's laughing because he won't let himself cry. Look at the rest of them."

Drau was right. Vamma was weeping; others were wiping their eyes and clearing their throats forcefully.

"Bring him to me," Zerna said.

"I think this one is a she," Canly said.

"Give her to me."

"Only family, is it?" Canly said, walking toward her. "What a proud bunch of bastards you lot are. Or were, I should say. The rest of them are staying far away from this business, aren't they?"

Zerna held out her arms. "She's mine. Give her to me."

"Only if you call me Uncle Canly."

"What?"

Canly shook his head. "I was against this from the first minute. But it's done now. Once we've got everybody out–by the way, it looks there are about ten, so that's not too bad, I guess–we're going to break the vault into little pieces and then bury the pieces. So we can't go back. Your boyfriend here–sorry, your husband–married into your family. Two people taking care of ten or so helpless, mindless–I hope–creatures is better than one doing it all by herself. But you'll need help. Breaks once in a while. Babysitters. Respite caregivers. And if you will accept only members of your family as good enough to give you a hand, well then, there is more than one kind of family." He passed the first freed prisoner to Zerna. She took the withered woman carefully, supporting her head, and knelt on the broken ground at the edge of the pit. Zerna stroked the woman's face, murmured in her ear, rocked her.

"Another one's almost ready to come out," a digger shouted.

"I'll take that one," Fonell told Canly, who nodded.

Fonell crouched next to Zerna. "Canny old Canly, eh?"

Zerna shook her head. "Fonell."

"What?"

"I love you. I forgot to say that."

Vamma and another woman came up to them, with old bath towels–probably the quickest thing they could grab–to cover the released prisoner, and a bowl full of bits of cut up fruit and another bowl with soup in it, and smaller bowl of soft cheese curds. Fonell took all these things and set them on the ground, except for one towel, which he draped over the woman Zerna was holding. "Thank you," he said to Vamma and the other woman.

"We heard what you said about transportation," Vamma said. "Don't worry. My son has a van. Once they're all out, we'll drive them to your place."

"Thank you." He wanted to say Aunt Vamma, but he didn't dare.

Canly brought Fonell the second released prisoner. This one was smaller than the first, and male. The whole household punished for the crime of one, everybody–adolescents, children, probably servants as well. Fonell sat down, cross-legged, and Canly laid the creature in his lap. He felt cold and hard, almost like a corpse in rigor, except that his mouth was moving. Canly picked up a towel from the pile on the ground and tossed it over what had probably once been a teenager. "It might be another hour or so before we get the rest out. The vault is deeper than we thought. But I hear a van's on its way."

"Yes," Fonell said. "Vamma told us."

Canly looked at the bowls of food. He sighed. "That's not going to work."

"Probably not," Zerna said. "But there is more than one way of feeding." She glanced up. "These two aren't crying anymore."

It was true. The ones that Zerna and Fonell were cradling had fallen silent. Their mouths moved, like lethargic fish smacking at air, but they no longer called for food.

"We're still going to try," Zerna continued. "We'll run through the entire catalog of edibles in the world, to be absolutely certain. But this sort of feeding," she stroked the woman's face again, "might be enough to give them peace."

"I hope you're right. Still, it's a lot of work for just two people."

"Family of birth, family of marriage, family by adoption, which under the Code of Padrel the Great held the same status as family of birth, and family of choice."

"We'd be going for that last one there, girl."

"So I thought."

"Glad to hear you've been thinking about it. Have you decided?"

"Why would you do this?"

"For the same reason as you. It has to be done."

"Uncle Canly," Zerna said, "I will agree, but only if you endow me with the right to terminate the fictive relationships unilaterally and without penalty to either party."

"So many big words."

"All of which you understand."

"I do," Canly said. "And I agree to your conditions. I'll explain them to the others a little more simply."

"Thank you, Uncle Canly."

The neighborhood was the neighborhood. People took care of each other and looked after their own. Except when they didn't. But this was going to be one of the times they did. Fonell felt humbled, and proud of his people.

"You were going to be a lawyer," Fonell said, when Canly had gone back to the excavation.

"Maybe. Now I'm going to be something else. What about you?"

"Me? Nobody special. I'm still working at the warehouse. Probably I should say I was working at the warehouse. I suppose I'm going to be something else now, too."

"We're going to be something else together."

"Together, and not alone," Fonell said, gently. The curled-up creature on his lap stirred, and he stroked the boy's head. "You have in-laws too, now, remember. In-laws count as family."

"I was always going to come back. That was what my family–my birth family–didn't understand."

"I knew you would."

"Do you think the gods play with us? That this is how they whittle away the boredom of eternity?"

"I think the gods don't care. Sometimes people do, though."

"Third one coming!" Canly called.

"I'll take him," Drau said, sitting down next to Fonell. "That is, if you don't mind, Cousin Zerna."

Laugh to stop yourself from crying. Fonell couldn't laugh, but he forced himself to grin. Glancing at Zerna, he saw that she had gone him one better–she was smiling and weeping at the same time. "It's going to be all right," Fonell said.

"It's going to be what we make of it."

"And we'll make it all right. Together, and not alone."

"Sounds like a plan," Drau said. He pulled the bowl full of cut-up bits of fruit closer to him. Fonell raised his eyebrows. Drau shrugged. "The seal was broken. Maybe the magic can be broken, too."

"Don't get your hopes up too high," Zerna said.

"I won't. Just high enough," Drau said, and took another towel and spread it on his lap, ready to receive the third freed prisoner that Canly, shaking his head and laughing softly, was carrying toward them.

THE GARDEN

Carlea Holl-Jensen

Carlea Holl-Jensen was born on a Wednesday. Since then, her fiction has appeared in *Lady Churchill's Rosebud Wristlet*, *Underwater New York*, *Queers Destroy Fantasy!*, and *Fairy Tale Review*. She holds an MA in Folklore from Indiana University, Bloomington, and an MFA from the University of Maryland, College Park.

The air in the garden was green. That's what I remember most clearly: the air hanging between the trees, so thick I could have reached out and touched it. At the edge of the garden, tendrils of roses stung one another in the breeze.

"Come on, lazy!" Albie called to me. "It's your turn!"

I took my shot, but it went wide.

"Bad luck," Albie said. His strike was as loud as a tree snapping in half. His ball hit mine, sending it flying over the grass and out of bounds. "Roquet!" he cried. "Bonus shot for me!" He struck again, sending his ball through the last two wickets in one shot. "Poison! Better watch out!" Albie always wanted to be poison instead of finishing the game. Why should he want it to end? He was having such fun.

"Can't we just say you won?"

Albie's expression went severe. Then, just as quick, it softened. "Just this once, I suppose." He flung his mallet away and flopped onto the ground.

The grass was soft under my cheek when I lay down next to him. "Thank you, Albie," I said, more to the clover than to him.

I called him "Albie", or "Percival", his middle name, or "brother dear" or "my white knight", and he called me

"Evelyn", because that's my name. I used to call him "my turtledove", a pet name someone had given him once, but I stopped after he told me that doves were really just ugly old pigeons, anyway. Besides, Albie is more like the kind of white doves people keep as pets—very pale. His hair is so pale it has a slightly pinkish cast. Even his eyelashes are almost transparent. His eyes are the only part of him that isn't pale. They're like a dove's, too—black-black, so black it's hard to tell them apart from the pupil.

"It looks like rain," I told him. The clouds were gathering big and sickly grey.

Albie snorted. "It won't rain."

And it didn't. We lay watching the clouds crawl by for an hour or more. I tried to remember the names of all the different types of clouds—cirrus, nimbus, cumulus, stratus. Nimbostratus for steady rain and towering cumulonimbus for thunder. Altostratus, a grey transparent haze, and cirrostratus, which makes a white ring around the sun. Albie pointed out one cloud that looked like a dragon, another that looked like a water buffalo. The sky darkened and I held my breath for the rain, but Albie just kept talking—there's a castle, he said, and there's a dog—and finally the storm passed without becoming a storm at all. Just as he knew it would, the air thinned out and the sun appeared. I never should have worried about the rain, not when Albie said it wouldn't come.

"Which one is your favorite?" Albie gestured up toward the sky. "Pick one."

I looked for a long time. I've often wished I could rise up and walk amongst the clouds, so soft and fine and stretching on forever beyond the horizon. It would be like going along an endless corridor. With the storm banished, all the clouds that afternoon were fresh and very clean. They were all so lovely, it was hard to pick just one, but the one I liked the best was a soft, fat cumulus with a vulnerable pink underbelly. "That one," I told Albie.

"Then that's the one we're going to keep," he said. "I'll carve our names in it, 'Albie and Evelyn forever', and it will stay with us always." He gave me a swift kiss on the cheek and sprang to his feet. "Let's go have supper, I'm starving!"

We ate at the kitchen table—ham sandwiches and milk. Then we went out onto the veranda and ate ice cream from Albie's favorite silver bowls. We were celebrating, he announced— celebrating just the two of us, the garden, and our very own cloud. "Why shouldn't we celebrate?" he said.

After ice cream, we played several games of Snap on the veranda, then watched the stars come out. When we were both yawning too much to talk, Albie declared it to be bedtime.

Albie lay down next to me in our little bed in the old nursery and pulled the humid sheet over our heads. I lay still, watching him in the half-dark, waiting for him to tell me about all the things we were going to do the next day. He would always rehearse every last detail, deciding what we'd eat for breakfast and the color of the sky. Once he said there would be fireworks and there were, just visible over the horizon, pure sparks of color flaring up over the trees.

"We'll wake up early tomorrow," he said, "and have oatmeal with strawberry jam, and then we'll play blind man's bluff. Our cloud will stay put and the hellebore will start to bloom. After luncheon, we'll go swimming, and there will be roast chicken for supper."

His steady recitation of the events of the day to come reminded me of a song someone used to sing to us at bedtime. When his predictions were done, Albie made the light go and we fell asleep.

We woke at the cusp of dawn. Breakfast was waiting for us

when we went down—oatmeal with strawberry jam, Albie's favorite. He licked the back of his spoon and grinned at me, his teeth red. I ate around the jam because I don't like the way the seeds feel between my teeth.

As soon as he was done, Albie ran out to check on our cloud. Just as he promised, it was waiting right where we left it. It swayed slightly on the breeze but did not stray from where Albie had fixed it, as surely as if it were anchored by some invisible thread.

And just as Albie had predicted, there was hellebore blooming in the garden, its flowers reddish-purple, so dark they were almost black. I made a promise to look hellebore up in the encyclopedia later, so I would know everything there was to know about it.

Albie handed me a strip of cloth and said, "You're it."

In the gauzy dark behind the blindfold, I stumbled across the uneven ground with my arms outstretched. The garden seemed so big with my eyes closed. Albie could have been anywhere. I imagined him standing just out of reach, watching me.

Albie was always watching me. He was always warning me back when there was something sharp on the ground, telling me to watch my step on the stairs. They're very steep, the stairs, and I have a fear of falling down them. I did once, the winter I turned six. I broke my arm in three places and the bone stuck out of my skin like a new tooth. Albie was watching me then, too. Even now I know he's watching.

I have never been even half as good as Albie at noticing things. Whenever it was my turn to be It, I took ages to find him, but whenever he was It, he found me in a heartbeat. He said he could hear me breathing, or that my dress made a certain sound. When I was It, though, I couldn't hear anything but the wind in the trees and the mourning doves cooing in the distance somewhere.

Before long, Albie got tired of blind man's bluff. "It's too easy," he said. I wondered if it was so easy for Albie because he peeked, but I couldn't bring myself to believe that he would ever cheat. Now I think maybe he didn't have to.

***

I was hoping Albie would forget about going for a swim that day, but sure enough, after luncheon he announced it was time to go swimming.

"Can't we do something else?" I asked.

I hate the pool. It's too deep, too still for me to trust it completely. Albie loves swimming but hates to swim alone.

"If you really loved me, you wouldn't make me swim by myself." Albie narrowed his eyes at me. "What if I drowned? Then you'd be all alone and it would be your fault I was dead."

In the end, Albie let me sit on the edge of the pool and trail my legs in the water while he swam laps. With his pale, pale hair and green bathing suit, he looked like a calla lily cutting the water. It made me nervous how long he could go without coming up for air, and also how the water made the edges of him indistinct.

"Why don't you come in?" he asked, leaning his thin, white arms next to my knees. His hair was slicked back against his scalp, smooth as a polished skull.

"I don't have to if I don't want to," I said.

"Yes, you do." He reached out and pulled my ankle, jerking so hard that I almost fell into the water. I screamed and flailed, trying to resist. "Just kidding," he said, releasing my leg. He pushed back from the wall of the pool and coasted away, laughing.

The backs of my thighs were all scraped up from the slate tile along the edge of the pool, but I knew if I told Albie, he'd call me a baby for complaining. And anyway, I reasoned, Albie didn't mean to hurt me. He liked to play rough sometimes, that was all.

When Albie was finished swimming, he climbed out of the pool and lay down in the sun to dry. I sat beside him, twisting clovers between my fingers and watching the slow rise and fall of Albie's chest. It was hot, as if the day was trying to squeeze in all the heat it could before it had to concede to evening. The clouds were moving across the sky with elaborate languor. Never had clouds moved so slowly. I tried to count the number of breaths it took one of them to cross the lawn, but I lost count.

"You're getting pink," Albie said, and all at once I could feel the tightness of sunburn across the tops of my cheeks. "Why don't we go inside until supper?"

"Can we go to the library?" I asked.

"All right, if you like." Albie never cared about books, but he was willing to indulge me.

Before we went inside, he made me brush away the tiny blades of grass scattered across the planes of his back. They stuck to his skin, leaving little impressions like inverse welts once they were gone.

***

The library is my very favorite room in the house. Now it feels like the only room, but it has always been the best, in my opinion. It's always sort of twilight inside and the bookshelves go all the way to the ceiling. It reminds me of someone tall sitting beside me, a soft voice helping me sound out a difficult word.

Albie slumped in a chair, leafing through an old magazine while I looked up hellebore in the encyclopedia.

I love flowers, and pictures of flowers even better. That's why I like the illustrated encyclopedias best. I like animals, too, but I don't prefer pictures of animals to the real thing. No drawing I've ever seen of an animal has ever remotely resembled the creature it was supposed to be. They always seem mangled, misshapen. Drawings of birds always look like their necks have been wrung, and I hate even to think of dead animals. That's why I prefer flowers, because even though cut flowers die in time, for a while they're still as lovely as when they were alive.

"Did you know," I told Albie, "that hellebore is a member of the buttercup family?" The encyclopedia's pages were slippery-smooth under my fingers, the writing so small it was difficult to read.

Albie flipped a page in his magazine, pretending he couldn't hear me.

"And did you know it's winter-flowering?"

Albie looked up then, annoyed. "So?"

"Nothing." I turned the page idly. Several pages later was an entry on hematite, or ferric oxide. "Albie," I said, "who do you think writes encyclopedias?"

"Why does it matter who writes them?" I could tell he was getting impatient with me.

I tipped my head to the side, considering. "Do you think it's one person who knows everything about everything in the world, or is it lots of people who only know a lot about one little, particular thing?" Albie didn't answer, only slumped lower in his chair. "I wish I knew everything about everything. I think that would be better than just knowing a lot about one thing, don't you?"

"You know everything about the garden, and the house, and

me. What else could you possibly want to know?" Albie's voice was sharp and I felt as though I'd betrayed him somehow, and betrayed the garden, too.

"Nothing, Albie." My eyes were pricking with tears. "Nothing, never."

Albie was silent and still, his expression dark—jealous, I realize now, though then I believed I had hurt him. I fell at his feet, clinging to his legs like I used to when we put on stage plays and he was the knight and I was the maiden he'd saved from a dragon. "Oh brother dear, please forgive me," I cried. "Please don't be cross with me. I'll never leave you, I promise."

He was smiling despite himself. "Swear?"

I clasped my hands to my chest. "Upon my life!"

He laughed then. "Come on, silly, it's time for supper."

And just like that, his temper was over. He let me hold his hand on the way to the kitchen. I always hated it when Albie was angry with me and would do just about anything not to be in a fight with him. I thought we should never be divided, that it was supposed to be the two of us together always.

We found roast chicken and buttered rolls waiting for us in the kitchen. We ate with our fingers.

"Aren't we supposed to eat supper in the dining room?" I asked.

Albie frowned. "When did we ever do that?"

I tried to recall. For a moment, I had been so certain that we had—with the good china and candles on the table and the cut crystal cruet set. I thought I remembered someone telling me to put my napkin on my lap. But when I tried to picture it, it seemed half-realized, as if I were just inventing it. "I don't know."

Albie put a piece of pale pink meat between his teeth. "I don't think we ever did that," he said, chewing delicately. "Now finish up your milk."

At bedtime, Albie promised we'd have my favorite for breakfast and in the morning there was orange marmalade. We ate it right out of the jar and Albie said, "See? What did I tell you?" I didn't tell him that orange marmalade only used to be my favorite, and my new favorite was honey on toast. After all, orange marmalade was still my second favorite and I didn't want to hurt his feelings.

After breakfast, we checked on our cloud. I wondered whether it minded staying with us. Maybe, I thought, it would rather go somewhere else, but when I asked Albie, he said, "But where else would it go?" I couldn't think of an answer.

"I just think maybe we should do something nice for it," I told him. "So that it knows we love it."

Albie agreed, and we had a special tea in its honor, with lemonade and candied violets for appetizers and potted shrimps for the main course. Albie composed a poem about how much we loved the cloud and I sang it a song.

We were just finishing up when the sky went dim and it began to rain. Albie hadn't predicted the rain, but when I pointed that out, he went all still and wrathful.

"Why don't we play hide and seek?" I said. Water was pearling in Albie's hair and I had the feeling that if we didn't get inside soon, something terrible would happen.

I felt a little easier once we were inside, although it didn't last.

"Close your eyes and count one hundred," Albie said, and then I was left in the dim foyer, hiding my eyes behind my hands. I couldn't even hear his footsteps receding across the marble foyer.

I counted to a hundred, and then a little further. It was very quiet and a shiver ran through me to think of the whole house empty save for the two of us.

I started looking for Albie in the hall, where all the paintings are. Most of them are portraits of people but some are landscapes or pictures of horses. Some of the people in the portraits look a little bit like me. I wish I could remember their names.

Albie wasn't in the coat closet or behind the big chesterfield in the parlor. He wasn't in the dining room, either, its table laid with delicate blue-and-white plates. I checked the library, but even before I opened the door I knew he wouldn't be there. The study, on the other hand, was just the sort of place he'd hide, because he knew how much I hate it. It smells of tobacco and there's a taxidermied fox on one of the shelves that I can hardly bear to look at, let alone stay in the room with.

But Albie wasn't in the study, either. I trailed my fingers over the newspaper folded on the desk, and the glass ashtray and the letter opener. Trying not to look at the dead fox, I uncapped the fountain pen and scribbled a little nonsense shape on the blotter, feeling as though I was doing something I ought not. I checked under the desk and behind the curtains, but no Albie.

I took the stairs two at a time, because I thought Albie must be getting sick of waiting for me to find him. I looked in the nursery first, just to be sure, but I knew he wouldn't hide there. The other bedrooms were much more likely. We hardly ever went into them.

I searched the red room with the gold wallpaper and the blue room with its squeaky mattress and the yellow room with the doll arrayed on the bed. I could have sat all afternoon admiring the doll's soft mohair curls and her big silk skirt spread out like a fan. The yellow room is my favorite, or next to it. The best room of all is the big bedroom, with its green silk wallpaper and curtains embroidered with flowers and fruit. A silver hairbrush and mirror stand on the vanity, and cufflinks rest in a little silver bowl on top of the dresser. The clothes in the wardrobe smell familiar, a spicy, sweet tangle I can never clearly recall once I've left the room.

It occurred to me then that Albie might not be in the house at all. Of course he would hide in the garden, I thought, when that would be the very last place I'd look.

I rushed along the hall, past the door to the attic and down the stairs so quick I didn't have time to loose my footing. I cut through the kitchen—he wasn't there, of course—and dashed onto the veranda. The rain was pelting down by then, striking-hard, so heavy it was like fog in the air. I could hardly see the woods beyond the garden.

A noise resolved itself above the tumult of the storm—Albie's voice. I could hear him shouting, but I couldn't tell where.

I ran out onto the lawn, far out into the middle of the grass, turning, turning, trying to follow his voice, and then I saw him. He was up on the widow's walk, his hands curled tight around the iron rails. The wind was trying to toss him to the ground.

I know I screamed, but the sound was swallowed up by the rain, and anyway Albie wasn't listening. He was shouting into the storm, calling out to it, his expression wild.

Then the rain stopped so abruptly it seemed to sting. In the silence it left behind, I could hear Albie laughing triumphantly. The sun came out, turning the garden gleaming bright.

Albie noticed me then. Chest heaving, he looked down and smiled wide enough to bare his teeth. "Looks like you found me."

There were things growing in the garden that had never grown there before. I hadn't noticed until then, or maybe I did notice and simply forgot. But once I started to mark the differences, they were impossible to ignore. Foxglove and fumitory had insinuated themselves in amongst the lavender and bee balm and chamomile. Around the base of my favorite dogwood, big and gangly and good for climbing, clusters of sweet pea gathered, strained upward around its trunk like an anxious crowd. In the kitchen garden, bleeding-heart and lily of the valley rose out of the beds of mint and basil and sage.

The garden was blooming all out of season, I realized. Hellebore is winter-flowering, but there it was, not far from the lily of the valley, which blooms in spring. Sweet pea and fumitory are annuals—but nobody had planted any seeds. Was it Albie, I wondered, digging furrows in the dirt when I wasn't looking? I had a vague memory of someone, a kind-faced boy in a soft-brimmed hat, who helped tend the garden.

"Albie," I said, meaning to ask about the boy.

"Yes, Evelyn?"

He turned his head to look at me, fixing me in his dark gaze. I remember I had a dream once that I was walking in a dark room, and the dark of the room was the dark of Albie's eyes.

"Nothing," I said.

Albie flopped over onto his side and said, "Come on, I'll push you on the swing."

The cherry tree was in full flower and heavy with fruit so ripe it was dropping from the branch. The birds were doing their best to eat it up, but the grass was clotted with the red pulp of crushed cherries and buzzing with intoxicated wasps.

The swing creaked as I climbed onto it, bowing the branch above. The wood of its seat had grown porous and soft, the varnish all peeled off. I could remember someone—a woman—telling me something as I sat on the swing.

Albie rushed up behind me and shoved me hard, and the

swing jolted forward, flying into motion. My legs lifted as the swing rose, and rose, and rose. And then, finally, my momentum changed and I was pulled back.

"Albie, you startled me," I said.

Albie didn't answer. He was too focused on pushing me forward with all his strength. We settled into a rhythm—flying forward then reeling back.

I was trying to remember what the woman had said to me that day, but I couldn't. I remembered her dark hair, and the lean shape of her hands, which made me think of the silver hairbrush in the green bedroom. The woman and I were talking about my going somewhere, a trip, or some other place I was meant to stay. The memory was charged with excitement, but reflection, I was only confused. Where else could I have been going?

Albie shoved at me again when I drew close to him, casting me back in the direction that I came. His palms pressed against my shoulder blades, forcing me higher and higher. The air whipped around me, lifting me.

It was somewhere I would go to have lessons, I thought. I remembered then that we used to have lessons, Albie and me, but then they stopped. I used to like them, but Albie didn't.

I could sense the branch of the cherry tree above me, so close I might have hit my head. "Albie," I said, wanting to warn him.

Albie only pushed harder, throwing his whole weight behind me.

Every time I changed direction, the branch shook, aching to snap. "Albie," I said again, louder this time, but he didn't listen.

I gripped the ropes tight and held my breath. I tried closing my eyes, but that only focused the seasick feeling in my stomach. Every time I swung backward, I could feel my body pulling away from the swing, threatening to send me toppling to the ground. I wasn't in contact with the tree anymore or even hardly the swing, only with the air and Albie's hands.

"Albie, stop!" My voice was shrill, scraping at my throat. "I want to get down."

The pressure of his palms fell away and a knot of relief welled up in my throat.

Then the swing leaned back in his direction again and there was a sharp tug—his hands grabbing the ropes. The swing pulled up hard and dumped me on the ground.

My whole body seized up when I went down, paralyzed by the shock of the fall. I lay there in the grass, my chest jerking in panicked circuits as my lungs tried to work. I could feel Albie standing over me.

I tried to shape his name without any air.

He tipped his head to one side, his black eyes bright. I could feel him committing every detail to memory—the sprawl of my limbs, the red-dark stains on my dress. I wished I could hide from him. I wished I could make myself invisible, but there was nowhere he couldn't find me.

"I decide when you stop," he said.

I watched him walk back to the house, taking tiny sips of air while the wasps hovered inquisitively around me.

I knew I couldn't go back to the house yet, not when I might run into Albie. I thought I could just wait a little, until his temper had subsided and he was ready to let me apologize.

Until then, I wandered the garden, cataloguing all the changes I saw. The tall privet hedge along the edge of the property, I noticed, had lost its boxy shape and fallen into bloom, exuding a froth of white flowers. Yellow jessamine grew thick along the stone wall at the front of the house, almost entirely obscuring the gate. The front lawn was grown over with Queen Anne's Lace, so dense I could hardly wade through it. I reached down to pull a fistful of them from the dirt, and it felt good to clear the way ahead of me. But the more I pulled up, the hotter they stung my skin, until my palms were pricked red and blistering.

All at once, I was certain Albie was watching me. He was gone from the window by the time I turned, but I know he was there. I know he saw everything, his dark eyes wide and eager.

I wanted to cry, but not anywhere Albie might see me. I wanted to hide from him, and so I went to the only place I knew for certain Albie wouldn't be.

The library was cool and dim. I drew the shutters and curled up in one of the velvet armchairs and then finally I cried— for the garden, grown poisonous and wrong, and for the man and woman who used to sleep in the green bedroom, and for the lovely cumulus cloud Albie caught for me that would never get to drift off on its own, held as it was in Albie's sway. I cried until I cried myself asleep.

When I woke up, I was too hot and my mouth tasted thick, but my hands didn't hurt quite as much. I sat there poking at the blisters on my palms in the gloamy quiet of the library. All the shadows had expanded. Over the tops of the shutters, I could see it was the end of sunset.

Pushing open the door to the corridor, I stood on the threshold listening for Albie. I couldn't find the faint tap of his footsteps or the creaking of a door or the clatter of knife on plate.

"Albie?" I whispered, just to see.

There was no reply.

In the kitchen, I found the remains of Albie's supper still on the table: a tin of smoked oysters and a package of saltines, along with the browning core of an apple, picked clean. There wasn't much oil left in the tin, but it tasted rich to me. Standing at the table, not even bothering to sit down, I dipped one cracker after another into the oil, cramming them into my mouth as quickly as I could swallow them.

I didn't dare stay in the kitchen too long, lest Albie appear. Instead, I slipped back into the garden. Some part of me hoped that all the changes I'd noticed earlier would be gone, some cruel trick Albie had decided to play on me. I hoped he'd come laughing around the corner saying, "Ha ha, fooled you! You didn't think I was really angry, did you?"

Out on the veranda, the garden was draped in the last light of the day, whatever was left after the sun had disappeared below the horizon. Just beyond the rose arbor, I thought I saw a tall, dark shape approaching, and my heart caught in my chest. I was halfway down the lawn before I even knew I was running.

When I got there, it was only a willow sapling bending in the wind. For a moment I had hoped—I don't know what, but it was nothing.

That's when I noticed the smoke. It came crawling up out of the grass, clinging to the trunks of trees and obscuring everything it touched in a thin grey film. It had a sickly cold smell like ash, and my stomach turned just being close to it. The woods were filled with it, I realized, the trees choked with smoke, and I knew that Albie had put it there just for me.

"There's nothing else," said Albie's voice behind me, and I startled at his closeness, at his silent approach. Before I could turn, he wrenched my arm behind my back and pushed me forward into the smoke. I could feel it burning my bare legs. I was crying, but he didn't stop. "Want to leave?" His breath hissed into my ear and I tried to twist free. "Go ahead. Just see how far you get."

He dropped me then onto the cold grass, and I watched his shadow-shape disappearing across the darkening lawn.

Now I try to avoid Albie altogether.

It's hard to do, because he always seems to know where I am, and I can never predict when I'll come around a corner to see the white shape of him out of the corner of my eye. He seems like a stranger to me, his eyes the black, impersonal eyes of an animal. Often when I enter a room, I have the chilly certainty that he's just left it. But if I keep to the library during the day and I'm careful to lock the door and secure the shutters, I can pretty reliably stay out of his way. He knows where I am—he always knows—but he leaves me alone for the most part.

There are exceptions, of course. Most recently, he left a row of dead mourning doves across the threshold of the library, so that I had to step over them to get out. I cried for hours when I found them—their poor twisted necks. I didn't go out to look for food that day at all.

There isn't much to eat without him, but I manage pretty well. Sometimes all I can find are Albie's leftovers, chicken carcasses and half-eaten sandwiches he just abandons when he's finished, although often they've vanished by the time I can get to the kitchen. I've had some luck with the dusty shelves at the back of the larder, too—I found some dried apricots and tinned sardines there the other day—and there's a jar of Jordan almonds that someone kept here in the library.

Albie, on the other hand, has been eating nothing but ice cream. I know because I find his empty bowls in the kitchen sink, the pink residue of melted strawberry still sticky when I come in.

Going hungry while Albie gorges himself on sweets doesn't bother me so much, but now all the books have started losing their words—or maybe it's that I can't remember how to make the letters into words anymore. They linger just out of reach. If only looking at them were enough to absorb their meaning, like reading in a dream. At least I can still look at the pictures. Often these days I lie under the big table in the library and run my fingers over the heavy vellum pages of the atlases, trying to feel the contours of the continents with my fingertips, to sense the color of the oceans through my skin.

Everything is slipping away, everything changing.

The smoke presides over the garden. It pours out of the cups of poppies and seeps up from the covered well, roiling just above the grass. I can hardly go outside, because even when it's not near enough to burn me, the smell of it scalds my lungs.

Albie doesn't seem to mind it, or even notice. I've seen him playing out on the lawn, his arms flung wide like a hawk's wings, and he cuts through the smoke as if it weren't even there. He knows the smoke won't hurt him because the smoke is just for me.

Being away from him leaves me feeling thin, as though being separated from him has made me less substantial. Sometimes I think it's only a matter of time before I'll dissipate like fog. But even if that's true, I wouldn't take it back. Apart from him, I'm free to spend my days how I please—no more swimming or croquet or games of blind man's bluff. And even though some things are fading—the words in the dictionaries, the faces of people in pictures—other things become clearer, the longer I stay away from him.

I can almost remember the man and woman who slept in the green bedroom. More and more details about them come back to me every day. I remember her handwriting on my history lessons, the quick, sure stroke of her correcting line. And I remember his laughter, the smell of his pipe at night. And I remember Cook, who used to let us taste whatever we were having for supper—the most wonderful roast beef and chocolate cake and strawberry lemonade. They are coming back to me, but too late. They're all of them gone.

Albie has discovered he can control the light.

At first, I thought it was just another storm, but it was darker than that. When I went to the window, I saw Albie standing in the grass, poised like a conductor, and I watched as he made the sun set and the night roll past and then it was dawn. He laughed in sheer delight, and as he made it day and night again, I thought of those kings go mad with their own power and no longer recognize their loved ones for themselves.

I try to imagine how I might leave the garden. There's a road beyond the front gate, long and straight and leading through the trees—though to where, I can't recall. Albie knows, I'm sure, but he doesn't want me to. It goes away, in any case, if there is such a place anymore.

But even if I could cut through the thick vines that've grown up over the front gate, there would still be the smoke. The one time I tried to endure it—just to see if I could—I only managed to go a few feet before my skin started to blister. That afternoon, Albie willed the Northern Lights into the midday sky.

Lying under the library table, I try to remember the War of 1812. We had a lesson on it once, I'm sure, but I can't remember what it was about. Even as details of our old life become clearer, I've started forgetting other things at an alarming pace, not just words but places and people and dates—entire taxa of animals gone, entire countries. It's Albie, I know, slowly eroding little pieces of the world beyond the garden. I'm trying to hold on to as much as I can, but no matter what I do, it goes.

I mouth the words to myself, trying to sense their import: the War of 1812, the War of 1812. There is nowhere left to check.

The narrow printed columns of text in the encyclopedias are, at best, faint smudges. The War of 1812.

That's when stones start tapping at the windows. Cracking the shutters open, I peek outside. There are stones falling from the sky—not white hailstones, but flat, smooth river rocks, grey and brown and heavy. Albie's standing in the garden with an umbrella. The stones punch right through the black cloth, but they don't hit him.

Closing the shutters again, I turn off all the lights so that it doesn't matter what Albie is doing outside. I think he's forced the stars to change their places in the sky, but it's hard to be sure, because I can only remember half the constellations.

Even in their mutilated form, the books still keep me company. The field guides and atlases haven't lost their pictures yet. I still have the wren and the waxwing and the tufted titmouse like a small drop of silver water. I still know the Hudson Bay and the Straits of Gibraltar. These, at least, Albie hasn't taken from me yet.

I know he'll make those places go, too, eventually, just like he made the sun and the stars and the light in the nursery disappear. Some day, all the world beyond the garden will simply wink out of existence at his behest—just like the gardener's boy and Cook and the man and woman who slept in the green bedroom. He erased them, the same way he erases his dirty dishes after he's finished with a meal. I'll never see them again—I'll never see anything beyond the trees and smoke. Before long, it will be just the two of us, Albie and Evelyn, forever and always, on and on.

SERGIANE'S CHOICE

Melissa Ferguson

Melissa is a mother of two
and cancer-fighting scientist.
While her family sleeps she
thinks about cyborgs, cults,
zombies, enchanted woods,
future science, demons,
extinct species of humans,
evil scientists and infectious
diseases, and tries to mash
them together into awesome
stories. Melissa is currently
working on futuristic, post-
apocalyptic novel about cloned
Neanderthals. Her short stories
have appeared in *Postscripts
to Darkness*, *Page Seventeen*,
[untitled], and *Island*.

The high-pitched wail of a newborn resounded through the forest. Sergiane clutched the swaddled child to her chest and ran through the dark. Here and there the light of the just-past-full-moon broke through the leaf canopy or reflected off the eyes of some nocturnal forest creature. Leaves tangled in her hair and branches scratched at her cheeks. She stumbled over a raised tree root, threw her weight onto her knees to avoid crushing the child, and slammed into the ground. She stifled a cry and held her breath to listen to the thud of heavy feet and the snapping of twigs not far behind.

Breath tore through her lungs as she searched for a hiding place. There was a small hollow, just above her head, in a nearby oak.

"Calm." She touched her fingers to the baby's forehead and placed it in the hollow.

The baby shoved a fist into its mouth, closed its eyes and sucked furiously.

She steeled herself for Marvel's arrival. He stopped, gasping for breath, the knife she'd forced from his hand still in his shoulder. He grasped a tree to steady himself and smiled at her. It was the smile she'd seen so many times, a smile that had warmed her heart, a smile that, in the past, she couldn't help but return. Only now it meant something else and the eyes, above the familiar mouth, were different. They weren't the eyes of the Marvel she knew.

"Where's the baby, Sergiane?"

"Marvel, please. She's just a baby."

"She's an abomination. I need to feel her blood on my hands." He shuffled toward her, hands clasped in front of him. "She's evil. You must feel it too. This is my purpose in life, this is what my nightmares have been telling me. I must end this evil."

He lunged, catching his foot on the same tree root that had tripped her. He landed on his face and bellowed in pain. Before Marvel could move, she picked up a large moss-covered rock, dropped to her knees and smashed the back of his head. He grunted, put his hands on the ground and tried to push himself up. She smashed again and again, until his skull cracked and his wet brains oozed out onto the dirt.

Sergiane dropped the rock, put a hand on the rough bark of the oak and staggered to her feet. She stood for a while, staring at Marvel. His head was a bloody porridge of brain, bone, blood and hair. She'd killed him. Her man was dead.

***

2 years earlier

Sergiane hummed as she swept her cottage. The dirt eddied in the wind and settled into the shape of a face. A visitor approached. Goosebumps rose along her arms. She heard movement in the forest and leant the broom against the wall. The crunch of leaves and branches grew louder until a strange man emerged.

"Sergiane?" The man strode toward her.

He couldn't have been much older than her own nineteen years. There was nothing exceptional about his appearance; pale skin, brown hair, hazel eyes, average height and a thin, muscly body. She ushered him into the kitchen and sat across from him.

"You're a stranger to this island."

"Yes. A merchant seaman."

Sergiane nodded. "How can I help you?"

"Townspeople say that you're the woman to see about ailments. Name's Marvel, by the way." He smiled and reached across the table to shake her hand.

That's when it happened. The crooked curve of Marvel's mouth and the crinkles that formed at the edges of his eyes made her, for the first time, imagine being close to man. To feel his heat and weight against her. To possess his attention and concern. To not be alone anymore.

Sergiane held onto Marvel's hand for a moment longer. She followed the trail from her hand to his and up his arm to his face. Their eyes met and colour rose to his cheeks. She withdrew her hand.

"So, what's ailing you, Marvel?"

He sat back and rubbed his hands over his face. 'Nightmares. Every night I dream that a great swirling hole opens up in the ocean and the only way to save our ship is to throw a person into the hole. Then all the others—I can't see their faces in the dream—chase me. They toss me in." Marvel clasped his shaking hands together. "I'm falling toward the sharp teeth of the world when I wake up. It doesn't sound so terrible when I tell it out loud, but I wake up sweating and I'm starting to fear going to sleep at all."

"I'm no interpreter of dreams, Marvel." She liked the shape of his name in her mouth. "But I can make you an amulet against bad dreams."

"I'd be grateful."

Their eyes locked together again.

"Could you return tomorrow to collect it?"

"Aye. We're not sailing out for three more days yet. I think I'd like to see you again, before I leave." He looked at his hands and rubbed at an invisible patch of dirt.

She sensed that he had as much experience with women as she'd had with men and decided not to let the opportunity pass.

"Hmm…Perhaps you could give me the afternoon to prepare your amulet and then return this evening and share a meal with me?" Sergiane's blood rushed so noisily through her body that she barely heard his response. She did see him nodding and smiling with reddened cheeks. When he rose he knocked his chair over and hit his head on a pan hanging from the ceiling. She laughed as Marvel rubbed the back of his head. He laughed too.

***

Over the next few months Marvel crewed ships around the archipelago and spent as much time as he could with Sergiane. Within half-a-year of their first meeting they joined together in a simple ritual to prove their undying love.

Not long after their joining ceremony, Sergiane squatted over the cess-pit in her yard and whistled to a sparrow on the roof of the cottage. It had been well over one full moon since her last blood and her breasts were heavy and tracked with blue veins. She hadn't mentioned it to Marvel when he'd last had shore leave, she wanted to be sure. The summer sun warmed her back and she sighed as her full bladder emptied. She wiped herself with a square of moss, glanced down and saw a dark red smear on the light green. Her hand shook as she folded and wiped again. More blood. She threw the moss into the cess-pit, pulled up her bloomers and rushed into the cottage. She seized a jar of dried herbs, labelled *Bleeding in early pregnancy* in her mother's graceful script, from the pantry.

Fertility issues were a speciality of Sergiane and her mother. She'd prepared this particular blend of chaste tree berries, cramp bark, black haw, partridgeberries and oat flowers many times. Some miscarriages, she knew, were meant to be—an error in form or composition such that it was a mercy the child wouldn't be born—and some were due to imbalances in the body and upsets of the soul. This tea would only help the latter. She sipped her tea at the kitchen table and lifted her left breast, then her right. They seemed lighter, less pendulous and no longer ached at her touch. The baby had already left her.

***

Sergiane fell pregnant four more times. After a month or two each tiny life was washed away on a tide of blood. She called upon all her knowledge of midwifery; altered her diet; brewed special teas; made offerings to the spirits; chanted; prayed and wore her most powerful fertility amulets in contact with the skin beneath her slip. Even Marvel carried an amulet next to his heart and drank a brew to strengthen his seed. All to no avail.

At Marvel's suggestion they consulted an ancient, shrunken witch on the mainland, renowned for her expertise in fertility issues. They sat in her kitchen holding hands under the table. As Sergiane had expected, the witch's suggestions were remedies and charms she'd already tried.

"Have you consulted the spirits?" The witch touched her fingertips together in front of her face.

Sergiane blushed. "Well, I've tried. I'm not terribly good at it. My mother died before she taught me properly. I need more practice. I can call up faces, but I can't understand what they're saying."

The witch pursed her lips. "At least that's something I can do for you." She waddled over to a chest near the hearth and retrieved a little metal box. She dipped her index finger into the white, pearlescent powder in the box, brought her finger to her nostril and inhaled. Within moments the pupils of her pale blue eyes expanded until her eyes were deep black pits. She rocked back and forth, murmuring under her breath.

Several minutes later she came out of her trance. "I'm afraid it's not good news, my dear." She reached over to touch Sergiane's hand.

Sergiane pulled her hand away. "What do you mean?"

"You aren't meant to bear children. The spirits warn it could be disastrous to even try."

After that Marvel told her to let it go. He didn't mind not having children; he only wanted her. Sergiane wouldn't accept their childlessness. She'd come from a long, unbroken line of healers and had always envisioned passing her knowledge on to a young black-haired version of herself. She knew there were magical forces in the world greater even than nature. You just needed to know how to wield them.

Sergiane met, in secret, with a witch on the mainland who had a reputation for dabbling in dark and forbidden magic. The woman gave her a grimoire and showed her the appropriate ritual. Sergiane packed a deerskin bag with the items required and mentioned nothing to Marvel.

***

Several months later, while Marvel was away at sea, she stood in the kitchen mortaring leaves to replenish her jar of anti-impotence powder. She felt a gush from her vagina, clenched her thighs together and stumbled back to sit on a kitchen chair. She'd carried the baby for almost six months. Her belly had started to round and her hair had grown shinier and fuller. It was the longest she'd carried a child. Her womb spasmed and the life within her waned. The ritual couldn't be performed until the full moon, two nights away. She lay on her bed for two days, concentrating on keeping the tiny heart inside her beating.

When the moon rose on the second night she collected the deerskin bag and put her pet rabbit, George, in a small cage. Blood trickled down her thighs as she walked through the forest to the dandelion field.

The dandelion field was situated on a ley line—a place of great magic where the skin between the worlds is thin. She closed her eyes, held her palms out and wandered through the knee-deep dandelions, searching. She arranged a circle of stones around a spot where pure magic geysered up through a crack in the fabric of the world and sat cross-legged within the circle. From within the deerskin bag she produced the grimoire, a candle, a vial of seawater and a bronze dagger. She touched the wick of the candle with the tip of her finger and said, "Alight." The wick burst into flame. She wet her finger with the seawater and drew a vertical line in the middle of her forehead. Beside that she placed a smear of dirt. She put one hand on the grimoire. It snapped open to the ritual.

"I, Sergiane, harness the power of soil, wind, fire, water, hearts-blood and magic to restore and return that which nature has claimed."

Electricity charged the atmosphere. Her plait rose into the air. A high-pitched buzzing filled her ears. She took George out of the cage and held him by the neck with one hand. With her other hand she grabbed the dagger and plunged it into the rabbit's chest. She cut the beating heart, no bigger than a strawberry, out of the rabbit and placed it in her mouth. It slid down her throat, warm and slippery. She clenched her jaw to suppress a retch. Sergiane plucked a dandelion puff-ball from the earth beside her. The world disappeared. She sat in complete silence at the centre of the darkness.

"Child inside me, I wish for your return and restoration to what you once were and what you should be." She blew on the seed head. Dandelion seeds swirled in the air. Power from deep in the world's core surged through her, like magma through a volcano and brought life back to her womb.

***

Sergiane carried the child to full term. As the birth became imminent Marvel stayed with her.

The squalling baby arrived in the early hours one morning—with brown hair, like her father, not the curly black hair she'd always imagined. The moment the baby exited her watery cocoon she had an effect on Marvel. It began with scowls and angry mutters under his breath. Within a day of the child's birth Marvel picked up the kitchen knife with the intention of killing her.

***

The baby slept on as Sergiane lifted her from the tree hollow. The forest was silent except for the rustle of leaves and the creak of wood bending in the wind. The forest animals had been silenced by the brutality.

The baby wailed as they approached the cottage. Sergiane knew another calming spell wouldn't work and neither would walking around rocking and singing lullabies. Milk trickled from her breasts. The child had repeatedly refused to suckle, latching on well and then turning her head and spitting out the thin white liquid. Sergiane tried once more. The effort only incensed the baby further. She suspected the child hungered for something else. She placed the red-faced baby in her wicker bassinet and picked up a square of muslin. From the back of the cottage she collected a shovel and headed back into the forest, towards Marvel's corpse and away from the baby's relentless cries.

With a heave and a burst of power from within, she rolled Marvel onto his back. A sharp waft of stale sweat rose from his body. The knife was slippery with blood. She laboured to pull it out of his shoulder. Once it was out she sat back on her haunches to catch her breath. She leaned over Marvel and opened his shirt, button by button. She tried not to look at his face and kept her eyes on the black hairs which circled his nipples and the inked pictures which adorned his skin. Above his heart a big-breasted mermaid, with *Sergiane* inscribed underneath, gazed at her. She sobbed and remembered the times she'd rested her head against his chest. She drove the knife into his flesh and cut a deep gash. She found his cooling heart, used the knife to sever it from the attached blood vessels and wrapped it in the muslin square. She picked up the shovel and began to dig. She could have used magic, but she wanted to feel the blisters form on her fingers and her muscles ache with effort.

The black fabric of the sky had faded to grey and the stars were winking closed when Sergiane returned to the cottage, filthy, thirsty, hungry and exhausted. She didn't know which need to attend to first and barely had the strength for any of them. Her child's insistent need roused her. First she would prepare the heart.

She packed wool into her ears, fed the fire and put a kettle of water on to boil. The baby's cries pulsed dully through the wool. Sergiane unwrapped the heart, laid it on a wooden board and chopped it. Once the water was bubbling she poured just enough to cover the minced heart and left it in a bowl to cool. She brewed a poppy and liquorice root tea and mixed the rest of the hot water with cool water. She stripped off her soiled dress, stepped into the wash tub and scrubbed away the blood and dirt from her deep brown skin. No man would touch her skin ever again. Marvel had died so that the baby could live. He was gone. Unless… No, her affair with dark magic had ended.

Sergiane ate a hunk of bread and poured herself a mug of tea while the heart-broth cooled. She poured the chunky, black liquid into the square of muslin and tied it in a knot at the top. She held the muslin to the screaming mouth. The child began to suck. Her whole body relaxed, rocked every few minutes by a spasm of her agitated diaphragm. The baby's skin faded from purple-red to a pink-tinged ivory. Once the child had stilled Sergiane unwrapped her and removed a red-stained cloth from her chest to reveal a clotted wound.

She lifted the sucking baby out of the cot, inhaled the yeasty scent of the child's scalp and lowered herself into the arm-chair by the fire. She held the baby tight against her to ease the pressure in her leaking breasts and listened to the awakening birds and the crackling fire. Finally Sergiane closed her eyes and hoped the life she had chosen to save was the right one.

THE
KING IS DEAD

Miranda Geer

Miranda is a college freshman majoring
in middle school education. She loves
weird, gripping, mind-boggling science
fiction both old and new, and has been
writing her own for fun since the age of
ten. Animals haunt her dreams.

I found the snake one cold night when I was driving back from Korongo Wildlife Preserve.

Korongo is far from my home. I live in Kampala. It is a long drive in my old truck, but the pay and the work are good. The park rangers at Korongo say they will not have anyone else but me to help when there is trouble with the animals. They will only call me, even though there are other veterinarians who live much closer. Always, I am glad to go.

It is a long drive back to Kampala, but I do not mind. Driving is good when the moon is high and the air sweet. The road winds through the bush, empty and wide, only shrubs and bare ground on either side.

That night I found the snake , my truck rattled, and I hummed a driving song with the moonlight on my face. Sometimes I took a drink from my bottle of tea.

When I saw the shape of the dark thing in my headlights, I stopped. There are not many trucks on that road, but even so the animals sometimes are hit, and then they die because no one else comes. I took my bag of medicine and climbed out of the truck.

There was a gerenuk lying in the road. I do not know if you have ever seen one. They are tall antelope with long necks. This one was a female. She was lying down in the dust kicking her long legs and squealing. Her left back leg was not right.

When she saw me with my truck, she rolled her eyes so that the whites showed. Her nostrils were stretched very wide and small drops of blood came out of them when she exhaled. This made me afraid that she was hurt inside. Her muscles, which should have been soft and supple, were hard as wood beneath her liver-colored pelt. With her head and neck she was crying No! No!

I turned off my truck so that the light and the noise of the engine would not frighten her, and then I started to walk up to her very quietly.

I do not know you, she cried.

I did not answer. It is rude to contradict an animal when it says it does not know you.

Instead, I put on the thoughts of a gazelle, which I had taken from a dead gazelle at Lake Mburo. A gerenuk would have been better, but I do not have the thoughts of a gerenuk. I took the thoughts of the gazelle from the back of my mind and put them on top of my thoughts. Once I had put the thoughts on, my words were the words of a gazelle. I stepped lightly, my head high and my steps long. I breathed like a gazelle. I moved easily. The gerenuk relaxed, and she was not so afraid anymore.

I know you, said the gerenuk.

I know you, I answered with my neck muscles. This is not easy to do.

I poured a bowl of water from the water jug in the back of my truck, and to the water I added morphine. I placed the dish before her, near enough that she could drink without twisting her neck, for I did not know what hurts she might have taken.

I knelt beside the bowl, and lowered my face to it. I made

drinking sounds so that the gerenuk knew the water was safe, but I did not drink.

Good, I said to the gerenuk. *Good water.*

Then I moved back.

The gerenuk was very thirsty. She lifted her head and drank deeply of the water. The medicine took hold quickly, and she put her head down and went to sleep in the dust. I took off the gazelle thoughts because it is not good to leave them on too long, for they will grow roots. When these roots grow it becomes difficult to remain a man. This mistake I have made before.

I touched the gerenuk's side, but she did not stir from her sleep, so I put my hands on her crooked left back leg. The bone was not broken, but the hip was out of joint, and the limb was wrenched and sprained. I guided the bone back into place. Had the gerenuk been awake, the pain would have been too great for her.

She had hurt ribs also, but only one was broken, and she could heal them on her own. Her ventral side was gashed, and I took needle and thread and stitched the wound. Then I lifted the gerenuk in my arms. She was not heavy. I carried her a little way into the scrub then brought the can of petroleum from the back of my truck. When I found a deep hollow beneath the thorn bushes, I laid her down.

The branches would shield her from buzzards until she awoke. I poured the petrol in a circle about her, for the smell is offensive to all animals, and would keep jackals and lions away. Once these things were done, I returned to the road.

Always I have been able to wear the thoughts of the animals. This is why I am a good vet. Many people in Kampala or farmers from the bush bring their hurt animals to me. I must heal them, the crippled and the cancerous and scabied, because their pain harms me. I cannot bear their pain any better than I can bear my own.

The night was cool and had the noises of moving air and living things, and the moonlight was bright across my head. I did not want to drive again for a little while, and my arms still smelled of the gerenuk's blood. I wiped them with a cloth as I explored the road.

The road is different when you are on foot. When you are in a truck, the road is like a long river that flows from one city to another. When you walk on your own feet, you can feel the shape and nature of the land beneath, rising and falling and itching beneath the dust, like the muscles of an animal's back beneath the skin.

The road sloped down in this place so that it hid the road ahead, and often animals were hit. Only a few paces away I found a big porcupine, lying on his side in a big patch of dried blood with his quills pointing up. As soon as I saw him I knew that he was dead. He did not inhale or exhale, and the beetles were already in his ears. I touched him to see if I could use his thoughts, but his head was badly smashed.

When I was six years old, my sister's little cat died of the distemper. The dead cat lay beneath the tree in our rear lot all day long, for Mother and Father were not at home, and my sister and I were afraid to touch it. When at last we drew near to him, my sister poked him with a stick. I was close to her side, and I found I could feel the cat's thoughts still stirring in his cooling brain.

I stretched out my hand and touched the cat on the back of his head. While he lived, the cat was warm and soft and had no love for me, but in death he lay very stiff and cold, as it were wood and not meat beneath his pelt. I felt the bewilderment and anger of his thoughts inside his ruined body. They wanted somewhere to roost again, so I opened my hands and let them come. His thoughts flowed into me, settling in my mind. I put them on as easily as a skin, and then I saw as the cat saw and felt as the cat felt. Straightaway I climbed the big baobab tree and sat on the branch, and I found a nest of young plover birds. I ate them.

My sister screamed when she saw what I had done, but I wore the thoughts of a cat, and I did not heed her cry. Do cats ever heed such cries?

But here, the porcupine's head was damaged. There was no dwelling place for his thoughts, so they had spilled into the ground. I turned away to climb into my truck, but in the moonlight I saw something else.

A desert snake, dead perhaps a day. He was a large and handsome snake, striped on both sides, the color of bronze . His back had been broken by the wheel of a car, and he had dragged himself to the edge of the road to die. I knelt down and looked at him.

There was dust on his back, and dust on his snout. He had tried to dig into the dust before he died and I wondered why. His eyes were open still, and his body was untouched by insects. His mouth was open, the bright fangs glinting in the moonlight, his head undamaged. I wondered why he had come to this deathly road, when the land was so empty and good all around him.

The skin of his head had begun to flake off and blow away in the endless sun , exposing the glittering white bone of his skull. His thoughts were still inside his head because the thoughts of reptiles linger a long time after the animal dies. Perhaps it is because their blood is cold, and chills their soul to keep it from decay.

I once found the thoughts of a crocodile, still intact, in a bleached skeleton in a museum. The crocodile's thoughts were deep and slow, and they echoed. I did not take them. But here lay this snake. I did not need the thoughts of a snake because I have such thoughts already. I have the thoughts of a python, a water snake, a wolf snake, and many other kinds of snakes as well. And yet, there they hung, suspended from his open mouth, like a single drop of water that hangs, shining, from a damp leaf after a rainstorm. Do you know anyone who does not like to catch such drops in his hands? I do not.

So I took the snake's thoughts into my mind.

The instant that I did so, the earth began to shake fearsomely, and I fell to my knees. After a little while I realized that it was not the earth that shook, it was me. I shook fiercely. The snake cried out, and for a little while I could not stand up.

I climbed into my truck, shaking still, and began to drive, nodding my head to clear it. The snake had crawled to the forefront of my mind, and he was crying out over and over again.

Snakes are difficult to understand. This one was saying something I had never heard before. The first part of it was something like *master* or *king* or *strong,* but snakes do not say such things, for they are unto themselves and do not believe in leaders. The second part was *under,* and the third part was something more like *sleeping,* but that was difficult. Animals say the same thing whether they mean *sleeping* or *dead* or *no smell* or *gone,* and they do not use words as we do. I have to add the words by myself.

When I was a child, this was also the way that I spoke, and it was easy for me. I did not need words. Like an animal, I could understand the meaning in the twitch of a brow or a loud exhalation. In my ninth year, Mother and Father sent me to a school where they taught me to use words like people instead of like animals. Many things became more difficult after that.

I tried to put the snake in the back of my mind, but he would not go. Twice I almost drove away from the road, once I stopped the truck and waited until the snake had quieted somewhat. It was midnight when I reached Kampala at last.

***

My house is on the outskirts of the city. I bought it when first I went into practice. It is painted yellow, and there is an umbrella tree in the front lot.

The goats were grazing in the yard when I parked the truck. They lifted their heads and said *I know you* with their ears and front legs, and then they grazed again. I walked up the path to my front door, and they paid me no mind.

My dog was waiting at the door, and she cried *I know you*! and danced about my knees. I answered *I know you* and put my bag and coat away. My dog is from the police department. They found her and gave her to me. She has only three legs. Soon she will have a litter.

The mongoose was gone hunting, but I put out a dish of food for him. I fed also the fish and the monkey.

I lay down on my bed. Above me was the spider. She had made a web long ago, and because I like to see it I let her stay. She has grown large now, and she stays in the corner of the ceiling, her striped and crooked legs bent as she steps across her threads dragging a wrapped tsetse fly she has caught. I said *I know you* to her, but she did not answer. She never does.

I read for a little while, and then I went to sleep.

***

In my dreams, I crawled beneath great thorn trees in leaf. You have never seen trees like the ones I saw. They hid the very sky above from my eyes. There was a voice calling out to me, but I did not hear it in my ears. It traveled through the ground as stampedes sometimes do, and it rattled my body and moved it and buzzed it like skin of an eardrum. I heard because I *was* the ear.

Master.

The word awakened me. It was an animal's thought, tense and intimate, as I used to hear when I was a child. It was not as other animal's thoughts, and it did not speak like any other snake I had ever heard. It was not speaking to me.

The KING.

In the thought there was something like love. Animals do not love as we love, and snakes do not love at all. To love, my mother has told me, is to care for another thing as you care for your own body. How can a snake do this? It is difficult enough

for me, and my blood is warm. I was born from my mother's body, but a snake is born from a leathery egg. How, then, can it love?

"Snakes do not have kings," I said aloud.

The KING.

Far above me, I saw the spider rock on her web as she does when the wind is blowing.

I know you, I said to her. *Peace.* No foe.

The king.

"There is no king," I said again, but my own ears did not heed what I was saying. The spider trembled, though I wished to calm her. All night I lay stiff, my eyes wide open, watching her as she shivered. The moonlight fell cold on my face, but I did not dare to dream again.

***

In the morning, I dressed myself and made my meal, eating

it slowly with a fork as they taught me in school. The sun was bright on the windowsill, and the dog lay at my feet. The mongoose had not returned.

Before noon, a man came to me and knocked on my door, an English man with yellow hair. He had a parrot he had bought for his children. She was a fine gray one with bright eyes, but she held her wing as though it pained her.

The man told me he wished his parrot to be cured, and so I took her and carried her into my surgery, with the man behind me.

I spoke to the parrot gently, for she was pained and wishing to bite. I wore the thoughts of a parrot and spoke to her, with my eyes and my shoulders and small cries from my throat. The English man did not understand, but he said nothing.

The parrot was in pain, as I have said, but as I spoke to her she spread her wing so that I could see it.

There was an abscess in the wing, perhaps a scratch that had been infected. It was small but deep, hidden between the two joints of her wing. I told the man so.

He nodded, and then he lit a cigarette and turned his face to the wall. The draining of an abscess is not a clean thing to watch. I am able to do many things that are not clean.

The KING! Honor the KING!

The words stung my mind. The parrot screamed in sudden terror. With her wings and eyes she cried *Stop! Foe! Stop! Stop!* and she dug her beak into my hand. My hand bled, for the beaks of parrots are sharp, and before I could stop myself I hissed at her.

She began to cry out in Swahili: "Nyoka! Nyoka!" Gray parrots are good mimics.

The English man dropped a towel over the parrot so that she

would quiet, and he apologized to me for her behavior, saying that she had never done such a thing before.

I told him not to worry. I told him that I was accustomed to being bitten, and that a hurt animal will do almost anything.

This was a lie. I had not been bitten by anything in almost eight years.

When she was a little calmer I cleaned the abscess, but she would not abide my touch, and the English man had to hold her with the towel. She would not speak to me.

I gave the man a salve for the parrot's wing, and he paid me, and then he took her and went. She was still crying out, "Nyoka!"

When the man was gone, I dressed and cleaned the bite on my hand, and then I sat down and shook. The English man did not understand Swahili, but I do. "Nyoka" means "snake."

The King is waiting, said the snake.

Be quiet, I said to the snake.

The snake wriggled in my mind. He would not be still.

I fixed my lunch and ate it, and then I groomed the goats and saw to the monkey. The mongoose was still gone, and his food was untouched. I swept my floor, and as I swept it I tried to put the snake away in the back of my mind. The thoughts of this snake were not like the thoughts of other animals. They did not lie flat like a skin, they throbbed like a headache. I rested in my sunroom, and I dreamed. My dreams were of hot dust and

cold, bloody smells that I tasted in my mouth. They hurt. I did not want them.

In the afternoon, my sister Naomi came to visit me. She knocked on the door, and her knock is loud. I can hear it from anywhere in the house. I was reading in the sunroom, and for a little while I pretended that I could not hear her. But she knocked again, and the dog began to bark. The dog is with child, and it is not good for her to be stirred up. I sighed and stood up, and went to open the door.

Naomi had brought me a yam pudding. When she saw me, she cried "Francis! It's good to see you," and embraced me very hard. I do not like to be touched, and almost at once I pulled away and stepped back.

Naomi walked into my house and looked all around, to see if it looked well, and then she looked at me, to see if I looked well. When she saw the bandage on my hand she cried out.

"Francis! What happened to your hand?"

I told her that the parrot had bitten me.

"That looks awful. You ought to have a doctor fix it up."

I told her that I was a doctor, and I had cleaned it.

She snorted. "An *animal* doctor. Francis, why haven't you come to visit?"

I told her that I had been busy.

"Too busy for *us*? Rebecca misses you. Every day she asks me, when will Uncle Francis come?"

To this, I had no answer. If it were Rebecca alone who waited, I would be glad to go to my sister's house, perhaps every day. But David would be there. He is Naomi's husband and he smells frightening. Mother would be there also, and she wants me to live with her because she thinks it is not safe for me to live alone. But I *want* to live alone. None of this I could explain to Naomi.

"Your house is lovely, Francis. Will you show me around?"

Naomi says this whenever she comes to visit. She wants to look at my house so she can tell mother that I am not living properly, and so have me moved.

I told her that I showed her the house last time. I think she was surprised that I remembered this. "Yes…I suppose you did. Well, if there's anything you need, just let one of us know. Alright ?"

She touched my shoulder. This angered me, and I drew back.

The KING! He is MIGHTY!

The snake was in my mind, and his thoughts were my thoughts. I hissed, the hiss sliding from my mouth like water, and I drew my neck back to strike. I saw Naomi's eyes widen.

I remembered her when she was eight years old, poking a dead cat with a stick.

All at once, there was a snarling noise, quite small, the voice of an animal crying out, *P*REY! PREY!

There was a flash of brown through the dog flap, and then all at once the mongoose was on my leg, his eyes flashing red, his teeth fastened in my skin through the thick cloth of my scrubs.

Naomi screamed.

The sudden pain and noise brought me back from the snake's thoughts, and I knelt quickly, slipped on my gloves, and put on the thoughts of a mongoose.

"Hold still." Naomi swung her purse and hit the mongoose on the head, tearing him from my leg, flinging him to the floor. His small legs scrambled, and he reared up again, fur fluffed up in frightened rage, crying *Fi*ght! Fight!

"Leave him alone," I cried angrily to Naomi, and I spoke to the mongoose gently with my head and hands. *I know you*, I said to him.

His body flattened to spring, eyes narrow, the soft muscles in his back and jaw becoming hard killing things. *I do not know you*, he said, and then added Snake!

No snake, I answered him. Smell.

His eyes still flashing with suspicion, he scented the air. I saw the muscles in his back relax, and presently he agreed, *No snake. I* know you.

All this while, Naomi stood above me, her purse still held as if to swing. She turned furious eyes to me. "What is that?"

I told her he was my mongoose. "You hit him," I added. "His head is sore."

"He *bit* you. You're bleeding."

I looked and saw that it was true. The cloth of my scrubs was torn, and blood seeped from my skin.

I told her that it was a misunderstanding. This is a word I learned in my school. It is useful when you are in trouble.

"Misunderstanding?" She pointed at me, and her arm shook. "Francis—you live like—with…only these animals for company. What if you get hurt? It isn't safe. It's just like mother says."

I grew angry. I told Naomi that if mother wanted to spy on me she ought to do it herself.

"Oh!" Naomi cried out as though she had been bitten. "How can you say that?"

I looked Naomi in the eyes. This is not easy for me. "Did Mother not tell you to come?"

Naomi's jaw was tight. "Do you think that?"

I nodded.

Her eyes shone with tears. "She told me to come, yes, but that doesn't mean—Francis Hanssler, I love you, and I hate it when you float away from us like this. Why can't you understand that?"

I could not think of anything to say to her, so I nodded again. She turned and left, slamming the door so that the dog howled.

I cleaned the bite on my leg. The dog continued to howl. The mongoose crept across the floor and hissed. I felt the parrot's scream in my head, and my anger was a bitter gum in my stomach. I tried, once again, to peel the snake away, and I could not. It was like trying to pull my own skin off of the top of my head. It hurt.

* * *

I slept. That night I dreamed again of great thorn trees, and of an empty plain of cold dust that stretched out on every side. In my dream, the moon was shining, but my body was cold and the earth rolled by very slowly. The moon was bright, and a hook came up from the dust. I could not see the hook, but I knew without seeing what it was. It hooked itself into my eye and pulled. I sank into the earth and the earth filled my lungs and my nostrils. I was pulled into the earth like a stone sinking through water, and there was no light.

The pull was terribly strong, and I could not fight. I did not want to fight. There was no *I* to fight, only THE KING...

The KING!

I woke then, and sat up in bed. I did not rise quickly. I rose slowly and I was cold. My body was cold, though the

night was not cold. I touched my tongue with my fingers, and it was cold and stiff.

My room seemed strange to me, and I looked this way and that to see what was wrong. I saw the mongoose.

He was standing on my bed at my feet, and he was standing on his hind legs. With each breath of air he swayed. He made no sound, but his fur was up and his teeth were gleaming. With his ears he said Ready.

I know you, I said, or tried to say.

I know you, answered the mongoose, but the way he said it was a challenge and not a greeting, the way I have seen a hurt

boar greet a jackal before they fought. The mongoose wished
to tell me that he was not frightened, and did not fear death,
and he wished to spill my blood most of all. I have never
thought to see an animal greet me this way.

The mongoose jumped when I was not looking. He bit me
many times. I said, *I know you*, but he did not answer. I took
his scruff in my hands and pushed him away. He stood on
the bed, and there was blood on his teeth.

Snake, said the mongoose, *snake, snake*, SNAKE!

I know you, I answered, and touched the blood on my face.
At first I did not understand, but then I saw my eyes reflected
in the mongoose eyes, and then I understood. The snake
came upon me quickly.

The KING! Give him HONOR!

I hissed. I picked up the mongoose and put his head
in my mouth.

He struggled, fighting for all his life, and I could feel the fear
in his body, and also the rage. A mongoose will not die easily.
He was biting my tongue, my lips, the roof of my mouth. I
set my teeth across his neck.

Crush.

The voice was clear and cold, as though my own mind spoke.
I have never heard an animal speak so clearly. I have never
heard a person speak thus, either.

Bite.

My mind said *Bite* as it says *Breathe*. My mongoose once
killed a puff adder in my kitchen, but I bit all the same. As I
bit my heart cried out, so I did not bite hard.

My teeth sunk a little way into the flesh of his neck. He cried.

Crush.

No.

I opened my mouth and flung the mongoose away from me. I did not see where I threw him, or if he landed well. I heard him land. He was silent awhile, then I heard his small paws running away.

I spat into my hands—my blood, the mongoose blood. I growled like a lion, and I vomited. Then I lay down on the floor by the dresser and went to sleep again.

I slept longer, then. My mind was silent many hours. But long before morning the voice came again.

The KING is sleeping. When will he awaken?

The King.

The KING!

I awoke, and I cried out with the voice of a snake. My head was hot and wet. Above me, the spider trembled on her web, and my mouth was thick with blood. There was a little trail of blood on the floor, and the mongoose was not in the house.

***

In the morning, I did not speak to my animals. I flung their food at them from a great distance and ran away. The monkey did not like it, and growled.

I hung the sign on the door that says "I Am Closed." I did not eat. All day I lay on the sofa in the sunroom with the sun warming me. My head was damp, but I felt very cold. I could not

get enough sun. I heard no voice, but the sound of my heart was loud and it frightened me.

Late in the day, when the sun was red, there was a soft tap like a distant hoofbeat at my door. Rebecca knows I do not like noise.

"Come in," I said and Rebecca came inside. She walked

through the front hallway and petted the dog's head, then said hello to the monkey before she came to me. She was wearing a yellow dress and carrying a school bag, and her braids were tied with yellow ribbon. Her eyes were wide, and she gave me a look as if to say, *I* can come?

I smiled at her. It is not easy to do, but when I do it she smiles back, and that is good.

She did smile back. She has dimples, like Naomi.

"Hello, Uncle Francis."

"Hello, Rebecca." I nodded at the chair beside my sofa, and there she sat, swinging her feet. She wore pink sandals.

She kept silent for many beats of the heart before she spoke. "Momma says to tell you to come visit."

I nodded.

She bit her lip. "Are you angry?"

I shook my head. It is not easy, man-speech, and the movement made my head warmer.

Her smile returned. "Will Princess have her babies soon?"

Princess is what Rebecca calls my dog. I do not give names to animals, but I do not mind if Rebecca does.

I nodded. "She will. Her milk is flowing now."

Rebecca squirmed. "And I can have one?"

I looked at her, struggling to shake the snake from my eyes. "Will you be good to a dog? There is no one to stop you if you are not, and the dog will not speak up for his own defense."

Rebecca's brow furrowed. "I *think* so. You'd have to tell me how to do it."

I nodded. "I would be glad if you did."

She squirmed again. "Really?"

"Yes."

The chair creaked with her bouncing. She was like a wild deer when it is young and does not yet know to be afraid of a million hungry creatures.

"We're doing Egyptians at school," she told me. "They built pyramids for the pharaohs. Do you know about the pharaohs?"

I shook my head, and it grew warmer.

"Well, they ruled the people, and they had the heads of dogs and cats and snakes, and when they died the people wrapped them up in bandages and buried them down under the ground with all their servants and things, because they thought the pharaohs

would come to life again and rule them. Isn't that silly, Uncle Francis? Uncle Fran—"

I was shaking, I could not breathe. My body was colder than stone, and all was dark before me.

The KING is DEAD!

I hissed.

Crush, said the snake.

No.

I held my body rigid. I felt the air stir as Rebecca tilted her head, swung her pink sandals. I smelled her in my mouth, the sweet soap in her hair, the dust on her feet, the ink on her fingers, the hot, salty flesh beneath her skin. I did not dare open my eyes.

Bite.

NO!

Rebecca's voice was hushed, but not afraid. I was glad of that.

"Uncle Francis, are you being an animal in your head?"

I did not look at her. I did not want to look at her; I had serpent-eyes. "What do you know of thissss?" I did not want to sound this way, but I did.

"When you talk to the animals, you act like them. That's why you're such a good vet, isn't it? You can *be* an animal. Like Momma says. One time she told me about her little cat."

I moaned. The sun had sunk low, and suddenly I had no strength. My eyes would not open.

I heard Rebecca rise to her feet and pad over to me. Her voice was close to my head.

"Uncle Francis, your face is all torn up. Does it hurt?"

Bite.

Rigid and unwilling, I parted my teeth. I closed them. I parted them again.

"Don't worry, Uncle Francis, I don't mind. I think it's really great. About the animals, I mean. And I won't tell anybody. And, now I'll go home, okay? And I'll come back when you feel better."

She laid her hand on my forehead, her small, steady, warm hand, and for a moment I was a man. Then it was gone, and I heard her feet go away, and the door shut behind her.

The King is Dead.

The dog brushed against the sofa. I smelled the meat in her teeth and the milk in her belly. I lifted my hand towards her, for warmth, for silence. She snapped at my hand.

Snake, she growled. She fled from me, her belly dragging. I cried after her because I was very cold.

***

I went to bed, though it was bloody from my fight with the mongoose. I dreamed again that night, but I will not tell you the dream. I awoke with a sharp pain on my face. When I opened my eyes, dark bristles were in them. The spider had fallen from her web and bitten me between the eyes.

Crush.

My hand jerked before I could stop it, and my teeth snapped together. The spider was ruined, her delicate legs snapped and oozing. I felt the moist bitterness of her insides in my mouth. I swallowed. I spat.

I cried out. "I'm sorry."

Come.

NO, I answered.

I heard a story once, of a man who found a snake that was dying of the cold.

Come to the King. Serve the king who is buried.

No.

This man was kind, or perhaps he was only like me. He put the snake to his bosom to warm it.

Come to the desert. You and I.

"No."

The snake awoke, there against the man's chest. It bit him, and the man died. I suppose when his body grew cold, the snake died also.

Come.

"No." But snakes never die.

*Come to the th*orn trees.

"No." My own voice was weak. I did not understand why I was saying "no." I could not remember what "no" meant.

Come.

With my soul and with my mouth, I answered...

"Yes."

***

That was then. This is now .

***

It was not hard to find the place, and now I am here. The porcupine's body is gone, but there is a dark stain where he lay. The shovel feels good in my hands, and the dry bush-dirt moves easily.

The King is Dead.

My hands are not mine. Someone has stolen them. Where are my hands?

The King is Dead.

The snake is in my eyes. He is in my hands and back. He will not be silent. My spine writhes, my arms twist and curl as I dig. My spine is a snake's spine. My bones are snake-bones.

The King is Dead.

I dig.

When the moon is high, my shovel strikes something hard. On hands and knees, I scrape away dirt, clawing and scrabbling. My fingers bleed. Rebecca.

The King...is here.

The skull is huge, like a coffin, like a crown. I could be lost in one of the great eye sockets. As I scrabble and scrape at the dirt, the teeth appear one by one and gleam like stars. Though his body is buried, I can sense the shape. I will excavate him, resurrect him: the proud neck, the brutal tree-trunk tail, the short, cruel arms like a child's arms. I will bring him back from his tomb.

I cry, *Rebecca*, but I do not remember what is meant by the sound.

The king's head emerges, too large to comprehend. Even

the skulls in museums are dwarfed by it. They once ruled the earth, people say. Thunder lizards. A buried king. Rebecca. Rebecca.

The skull looks at me.

I know you, it says.

I do not know if it is me or the snake that screams.

THANK YOU

Many thanks to our patrons
and supporters, especially:

KE Jaeck

Tory Hoke

GriffinFire

Want to see your name here? Become a patron!

patreon.com/lunastation

ABOUT THE COVER ARTIST

Sara Kipin is currently a senior illustration major attending the Maryland Institute College of Art in Baltimore. As a child, she was gifted many illustrated fantasy books from her family and has now taken that inspiration with her into her adult years. Once graduated, she hopes to use these aesthetics as a book illustrator or a preproduction artist.

Learn more about Sara and see her work at:

http://sarakipin.tumblr.com

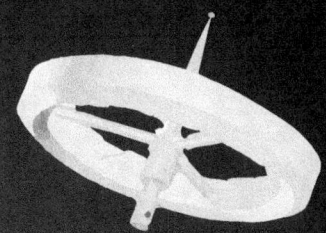